Sushi Scandal

A PRIDE STREET PARANORMAL COZY MYSTERY
BOOK ONE

T. THORN COYLE

"Klaus, Klaus, we have to get inside!"

"I know!" Klaus barked back. *"But I'm stuck!"*

"Calm down, you two!" Garrett said.

Calm down? How were we supposed to calm down? Couldn't they tell something was wrong?

"I'll stay with the dogs," John said. "You go see if Saschi needs help."

"Yes! We'll go help!" I said, but our humans didn't seem to understand.

Garrett just nodded and hurried inside, leaving us with John.

I gave a mighty wrench to my leash, breaking free and head-butting John's shin. Which was hard. Ouch.

No time to recover though, I had to take my chance, and raced after Garrett, Klaus's barks spurring me on…

For my Kickstarter backers, Patreon supporters, and for my strange and wonderful found family.
You know who you are.

CHAPTER 1
Marsha

MY NAME IS MARSHA. I'm a corgi, and my best friend in the whole world is Klaus. He's a corgi, too.

We were named after what our humans call "two queer icons," whatever that means. I'm assuming it means they were Very Important People, and since Klaus and I are also Very Important People, it makes sense.

We live in a very nice home, filled with gleaming wood, comfy chairs and beds, and a lot of art. And music. One of our humans, John, really likes music, even when he is "working now, please don't bother me."

But we're not at home right now. Today is a shop day.

Shop days are when Klaus and I walk our other human Garrett to his store because John is "on a publication deadline and don't have time to deal with the rascals today" day.

Since both the shop and home have soft beds, I don't mind. The only thing the shop lacks is a doggie door and a back garden. But what the shop has that the house doesn't?

People who coo over us, rub our tummies, and scratch behind our ears.

I like that. Mostly. It makes me wag my luxurious black tail. Did I mention my tail has a white tip? It does. It's very beautiful, like the rest of me. Klaus has a tail, too.

Sometimes all the human adoration interferes with my naps though. Like right now.

Klaus and I were snoozing on the big fluffy dog bed next to the big wood counter where Garrett did the books, rang up sales, and chatted people into buying things they didn't need, but really, really wanted.

I understand wanting things I don't need, because John and Garrett are always telling me I don't need another treat, or a new squeaky toy, or that they threw the ball fifteen times at the park and were tired.

Humans. They're always tired. I think they need more naps.

"Oh my gosh! These corgis are the cutest! May I pet them?"

I cracked open an eye and swiveled my ears.

The person looming over our big bed had short platinum hair that contrasted with their brown skin, rainbow striped sneakers, skinny black jeans and a black T-shirt with a big green heart in the center. They also wore makeup, the way John did sometimes when he and Garrett were going out.

Garrett never wears make up. And he always wears what he calls "proper pants" and nice shirts. He's shorter and softer than John, and nice to cuddle. John is taller, leaner, and more muscly.

"They both love a good tummy rub," Garrett said from behind the counter. "Hi Saschi! What brings you in?"

I looked past the person currently cooing at me. There was Saschi, standing tall in bright pink boots, black jeans, a pink T-shirt. Their shining, pale face was topped with turquoise hair.

"Yarrow loves mid-century modern stuff, and I told them they had to meet you," Saschi said.

Way to interrupt a belly rub. I licked Yarrow's hand, hoping they would stay. I gave the hand a lick and got a squeal in response.

"Oh! She…he? Licked me!"

"You must smell good. And that's Marsha, named for Marsha P. Johnson. Her blond sidekick there is Klaus. Named for Klaus Nomi."

"Not a sidekick," Klaus grumbled.

I tilted my head and preened. *"Face it, Klaus. I'm the one that people come to see."*

Everyone loves me. And why not? Like I said, I'm gorgeous. Black fur frames my eyes nicely, and I have tan and white accents for extra bling. Klaus is boring old tan and white, including his tail. I mean, he's still attractive, but not beautiful like me.

"Are not! Plenty of people come to see me!" He pushed me with his nose, then turned his big brown eyes on the human currently scratching behind my soft ears.

"Oh! Aren't you a cutie-pie?" The human turned their attention on Klaus, rubbing the spot between his eyes. He wiggled his butt and sighed.

Woof. *"Scritch stealer."*

Klaus didn't reply. The little furball was too busy cozying up to the new person. Saschi kind of hovered, as if they weren't sure if they wanted to be in the store or not.

"I thought corgis didn't have tails," Yarrow of the Rainbow Shoes said.

"Most Cardigan corgis do, actually," Garrett replied. "Pembroke corgi tails are traditionally docked. The original corgis were all working dogs in Wales, and you don't want a dog's tail getting caught in brambles when they're herding, or whatever. But since these two have never worked a day in their lives? Having tails is okay."

Hmph. I work plenty, but I was too busy getting my ears scratched to reply.

"But that was probably way more information on corgis than you needed." Garrett laughed. "So, what are you in the market for?"

Yarrow stood. I barked in protest, and Klaus whined.

"Hush, you two! I swear, they act as if they get no attention at all." I could hear Garrett putting on his I-have-customers voice. He doesn't like people knowing he's shy, but I can always tell when he's feeling overwhelmed. Garrett doesn't like attention the way I do, which is fine. More for me.

"I'm not sure what you're looking for," he said, coming around the counter, "but we have an entire mid-century modern area just for you. There's the most fabulous orange crackle-glaze lamp set I just have to show you! And of course, we have several chairs you might be interested in."

His voice grew more distant as he led Yarrow further into the store.

Saschi stayed. Crouching down, they took my face between their pale hands and stared into my eyes. "Hello, Marsha P. Johnson. How are you today?"

"I'm great!" I barked. *"Want to play?"*

I wiggled my rump, swished my tail, and crouched. Usually that was good for a game of tug or a ball throw. But Saschi just looked worried. And sad.

Also, they didn't smell right, and were kind of sweaty, even though I knew it wasn't hot out.

"Klaus."

"What?"

"Does Saschi smell strange?"

Usually, Saschi smelled like peppermint. Today? They smelled a little sour, like they were sick. And the peppermint smell was laced with old fish. My nose twitched. I mean, I like the smell of fish, but this combination was Not Nice.

"Old fish," Klaus decided. *"And mint. They're chewing gum though. And they do work at the sushi restaurant."*

I sniffed again, then sighed and relaxed under Saschi's ministrations. Chewing gum and sushi was probably it. But I'd never known Saschi's skin to smell like old fish before, even when they'd been carrying the little wooden trays covered in fish slices. Maybe they were coming down with what Garrett called a "summer cold." I guess that's different than a cold you get during winter, but I'm not sure why.

"I wish you could help me, Marsha," Saschi was saying. They were sitting on the floor now, face buried in the scruff of my neck as they scratched my head.

I gave a little bark to let them know I was listening. Humans like that.

"I'm in deep trouble," they whispered into my fur. "And I don't know who to talk to."

Uh oh.

"Tell Garrett!" I woofed softly.

"Or John!" Klaus's bark was louder. I swear, that dog has no finesse.

"They're good at helping people," Klaus said.

I had to agree with that.

Saschi sat up and gave one of those watery laughs that usually means a person is trying not to cry.

I heard Garrett and Yarrow of the Rainbow Shoes coming back.

Saschi dashed the tears from their eyes with their pale, slender fingers, smiled at me, and stood.

"I've got to get to work," they said, talking to Yarrow. "Did you find what you needed?"

Yarrow practically bounced in those rainbow shoes. I liked them. The shoes, I mean. And the person, too.

"Oh! Garrett has the most wonderful mid-mod chair that would look cute in my little living room!"

"Great!" Saschi said. Their voice was bright, but still didn't sound right to me. "See you around, Garrett."

"Sounds good. Maybe we'll come in for dinner tonight."

Saschi waggled their fingers.

"Nice to meet you all," Yarrow said, giving Klaus and me one final scratch, and then both humans were out the door. I looked at Klaus.

"What do you think is wrong?" I barked.

"With humans?" he replied. *"You never know."*

"How about it, you two? Want to hang out at Saschi's work when we're done here?"

"Saschi needs your help," I barked.

Garrett smiled. "I thought so. You two love that place, don't you?"

Then he turned his attention back to the computer.

Humans. Sometimes I think they don't understand anything at all.

CHAPTER 2

Garrett

PRIDE STREET IS my favorite place. Rainbow flags fly everywhere, shops and restaurants are filled with happy people, out walking and showing off their outfits, cruising, or sitting in bars and cafés, flirting or gossiping over tea or beer. Couples push strollers, toddlers shriek at the dogs tethered outside Leo's Grooming Palace, and the occasional drag queen totters by on heels that I can barely comprehend.

John can pull off heels when he feels like doing drag, but me? You'll never catch me in heels. Or a dress. Shudder. They remind me too much of my early years, when my mom still tried to force me into dresses and shiny shoes. I hated every second of it. Once I was old enough, I just started to refuse.

Our relationship went downhill from there. After all these years, I try to not dwell on it, but sometimes the memory still stings. You just want family to love you for who you are, you know?

At any rate, after the usual awkward phase of casting

about for my own personal style, I'm now your basic dapper man about town. I like fancy shoes and boots, my classic tortoiseshell glasses, the clean knife's edge of a sharp trouser crease, and vests over crisp button-down shirts.

I even wear the occasional bow tie if I'm feeling sassy.

Maybe it's being a trans man that makes me lean into classic menswear, but mostly? I'm just a lover of retro classics, both in furniture and personal style. You'll never catch me in John's jeans and T-shirts, for example, except for when I'm digging in the garden, though I've worn plenty of both in my trying-to-look-more-butch teens.

At any rate, we were ensconced at How We Roll, our favorite Pride Street sushi place. The fact that it's also the sushi restaurant closest to our house is a bonus.

John and I shared a two-top table set beneath the elm trees that dotted the sidewalk, providing the street with shade. Our corgis—Klaus and Marsha—were parked beneath us, snoozing, and probably hoping for scraps. One of their undocked tails occasionally thumped the patio pavers in happy contentment.

It was a beautiful early summer evening. Laughter from Axle's Bar across the street filtered toward the more subdued conversations at the restaurant.

Subdued, until a boisterous bustle arose between the planter boxes leading to the front doors. John and I both turned our heads to see who was causing the ruckus.

"The freaking Mayor of Pride Street," John grumbled. I looked around. Sure enough, there was Sweetheart Digs, a white man with dark brown hair, an always-the-perfect-amount-of-stubble face, and blue eyes currently festooned with rhinestone rimmed sunglasses that matched his silvery shirt. The shirt flapped untucked around brand-new dark jeans. Silver leather loafers peeked from beneath the jeans.

He wasn't wearing socks. That was a fashion that always grossed me out a bit, like going commando. I mean, didn't your feet get sweaty? And how often, exactly, do those commando people wash their fricking pants?

Not daily, I bet.

John frowned at the exaggerated I'm a Good Guy antics of the self-proclaimed Mayor of our little LGBTQ village. And John wasn't the only one scowling. Roderick Gauge pushed past the small group fawning over Sweetheart Digs. I couldn't see Roderick's eyes beneath his sunglasses, but his face looked like he'd been sucking on a lemon.

"What do you have against Sweetheart Digs?" I asked John. "I mean, sure he's kind of obnoxious, but…"

"We've got a past," John remarked darkly. "But I don't want to talk about it now."

I raised my eyebrows, but let it drop. This was news to me, but I trusted John. He would tell me in good time. Even life partners deserve a little privacy.

I turned back to the street and the happy, bustling people. The air rang with conversation and laughter.

"I swear, spring in Portland is my favorite time of year."

"I thought that was fall?" John teased. I smiled and picked up my paper menu.

Another thing I like about Pride Street? No cars. The three main blocks that comprise the heart of our little gay village are narrow and blocked to all traffic except pedestrian, with the occasional wheelchair or bicycle thrown in the mix. But bicyclists at least know to go slow around these parts. You never know when tipsy revelers might spill out of Axle's Bar or Enrico's club, further down the street.

Now, what to eat? I was in a nigiri kind of mood, even though How We Roll had gluten free tempura, which made me the happiest man in Portland.

But I was happier still to be sitting across from John, my Asian Lothario turned life partner. What the heck did he want with an awkward dork like me?

"Whatcha thinking?" he asked, catching my eye as he looked up from his menu.

"Thinking how lucky I am to have such a handsome sweetheart."

A smile lit up his face, dancing in his rich brown eyes, and crinkling his smooth gold-tinged skin.

On the surface, John and I couldn't be less alike. He's thin, with weight-trained muscles, has a shock of almost-black hair, and is a cis, gay, Asian thriller writer. Not that he writes gay Asian thrillers, but... you know what I mean. In his mid-thirties, he moved up from San Francisco over a decade ago, and still has a bit of that bigger-city sheen about him.

Plus, he looks great in drag.

And me? I'm a pasty, soft around the middle, early-forties white guy from nowhere Oregon. I'd had a penchant for interior design as a kid—the result of watching too many home improvement shows while hiding from the other children. I was also a shy, nerdy, boyish-looking girl with no tomboy skills whatsoever, except for woodworking, which was considered dorky. To say I was bullied was an understatement.

Add in that my parents had no clue what to do with me? Let's just say middle school was not the most fun time of my life.

Finally in high school, I discovered theater geeks who were happy to let me wear my jeans and T-shirts, or khakis and button-down shirts. They were just happy I was willing to build and paint sets. I was able to stay behind the scenes and still be part of something, which worked great for me. I also finally figured out why being forced to be a girl never made sense to me.

Turns out, it's because I was actually a boy.

John? Despite being a gay nerd, he was always popular. He's one of those people born to shine, which is why it cracks me up that he spends most of his time in his office in our classic Craftsman home, pounding out very popular thrillers on his keyboard, spending most of his time alone.

Meanwhile, my shop and design business both meant I had to interact with people all day long. But it's okay. I'd gotten used to it and figured out workarounds for the things that used to make me over-the-top anxious.

Also, social interactions with a function and a purpose? I can do those. Social interactions, like at nightclubs or parties? Uhh… let's just say I'm grateful John saw something in my soft, pasty self as I tried my hardest to fade into the woodwork at that nightclub six years ago.

One smile, and one dance, and I was a goner.

Still am.

"How are you two handsome men doing today?" Saschi, still in their pink T-shirt and black jeans, but this time with a black apron over it all, set down a steaming pot of jasmine tea and two delicate porcelain cups. Saschi was a force to be reckoned with. Their eyelashes and nail polish matched their turquoise hair.

"Great, Saschi, how are you?" John asked, smiling. "Any gossip today?"

"Can you turn that thing down, John? You're going to blind me!" Saschi mocked covering their eyes. John's smile was brilliant, and it wasn't because he had veneers. Unlike Sweetheart Digs. John was just charming and charismatic, and did I mention I wasn't sure how I ended up with him?

But something about Saschi seemed a bit off. First, they looked a bit flushed and were breathing heavily. I looked more closely, and despite their playful banter, there was sadness. And they had neatly sidestepped the gossip question, which was strange. Usually, Saschi loved to dish.

How had I missed all of this in the store? Oh yeah. I had mid-mod furniture to sell.

"Everything all right there, Saschi?" I asked.

The sadness was joined by a flash of fear, bordering on panic, but both emotions quickly fled, covered up by their usual friendly mask.

"Just fine! I mean, could this day be any more gorgeous?"

They were right about that. The spring rains had let up, and the sun was shining. Everyone seemed pleased as punch to be out and about in shirt sleeves after days and days of gray.

They were clearly uncomfortable, so I let it drop. We placed our order, got a dish of water for Klaus and Marsha, and Saschi went on their way.

"Do they seem off to you?" I asked. John nodded, pouring tea into both cups.

"Yeah. Probably just boy trouble."

"Probably," I agreed. Though I didn't believe that for a minute. Saschi went through men like they went through bath water, which is to say, they changed both often. I hadn't ever seen Saschi stay with anyone long enough to get heartbroken.

But you can't force someone to tell you what's wrong if they don't want to.

Soon enough, Saschi was back with our food, but again didn't say much, just hurried off after plopping down our rolls and nigiri.

The owner, Daniel, stopped Saschi at the restaurant door. Daniel is a handsome Japanese American man with graying black hair and pockmarks that only make his face more interesting. Saschi towered above him, but somehow Daniel seemed more intimidating than the waiter. The two exchanged some heated whispers. Daniel looked angry about something, and Saschi looked resigned.

Maybe that's all it was. Work trouble. And I'd be breathing heavily if I had to carry trays of food around, too.

I dug into a piece of dragon roll with my chopsticks, dipped it into wasabi soy sauce, and stuffed the delicacy into my too-small mouth. Then I groaned.

"I swear, John, if it weren't for the fact that our sex life is glorious, I would say this sushi was better than sex."

John smirked, raising his own sushi and tilting his head to admire the sunlight glinting off the tiny red jewels of flying fish roe topped with a perfect quail egg.

"Well, we can certainly put it to a test later, can't we?"

Oof. He sure knew how to distract me from my food.

We were halfway through our meal when the clatter of

a tray dropping in the indoor dining room, followed by a shriek, brought both dogs to their feet in attention.

Marsha barked and Klaus whined. The two corgis scrambled, tugging on their leashes and tangling themselves up in our chairs.

"Hey, you two!" John said, leaping up. "Careful!"

"Calm down!" I said, peering under the table. The dogs looked frantic. I crouched down to untangle the leashes from the chair legs, and Marsha yanked, sending John's chair crashing into his legs.

The dogs kept barking and would not be hushed.

So much for our nice, quiet dinner out.

CHAPTER 3

Marsha

"KLAUS, *Klaus, we have to get inside!*"

"*I know!*" Klaus barked back. "*But I'm stuck!*"

"Calm down, you two!" Garrett said.

Calm down? How were we supposed to calm down? Couldn't they tell something was wrong?

"I'll stay with the dogs," John said. "You go see if Saschi needs help."

"*Yes! We'll go help!*" I said, but our humans didn't seem to understand.

Garrett just nodded and hurried inside, leaving us with John.

I gave a mighty wrench to my leash, breaking free and head-butting John's shin. Which was hard. Ouch.

No time to recover though, I had to take my chance, and raced after Garrett, Klaus's barks spurring me on.

"Marsha, you're not supposed to come in the restaurant!" Garrett said, grabbing hold of my leash and stopping me at the door.

I just stared up at him, making my eyes big, willing him to obey my every wish.

It worked. Garrett relaxed his shoulders and sighed.

"How can I resist that little face?" he said. "Come on then, but stay close."

I tugged Garrett into the cool, dim light of the restaurant. It smelled like tea, furniture polish, and fish. Not the weird, fish-oil smell I'd gotten from Saschi's skin, but the delicious scent of fresh fish. My tummy rumbled. I wish I'd had time to beg a piece of tuna before the loud noise happened.

I trotted between tables of murmuring humans, nails clacking on the dark wood floors. Everyone was turned to the far end of the room, near the long bar topped with the glass cases of fish on display.

The music from the speakers was the loudest thing in the room, which was strange. Usually, humans eating and drinking things got very loud. The hairs on the scruff of my neck stood up.

Something very bad had happened. My corgi senses could tell.

"Marsha!" Garrett hissed. "Where are you going?"

I ignored him and followed my nose, and everyone's eyes, toward the foot sticking out from behind the long bar.

It was a bright pink boot that I had seen just moments before.

"Saschi!" Garrett gasped behind me.

Two people in white jackets and white hats were crouched near the waiter, who was splayed out between the sushi bar and a long metal table. A tray sat half on, half off their skinny chest, and their hands clawed at their throat.

"Get your dog out of here!" That was the owner, Daniel, growling at Garrett. I ignored him and trotted over, nosing one of the chefs out of the way. He made a soft grunt of surprise but moved enough so I could get near Saschi's face.

I sniffed around their face, but only smelled spearmint from the wad of chewing gum half hanging out of their mouth. And that fishy smell again, plus something sour.

It really didn't smell anything like the fish smells from the two chefs crouched nearby, but I had no idea what it could be, and why the smell was seeping out of Saschi's skin.

"What happened?" Garrett asked one of the sushi chefs.

The woman looked up and shook her head. Whipping the white hat off her dark hair, she ran a hand over her forehead. Under the yummy fish smells, I could smell her sweat.

"I don't know. One minute Saschi was chatting, waiting to pick up an order, the next, they were on the ground. I actually yelped, I was so shocked."

More like a shriek than a yelp, but I know better than to argue with humans about things like that.

"I did hear them throwing up in the bathroom earlier," the other chef said. "But when I asked, they said they'd just eaten something that disagreed with them."

I knew something smelled wrong about Saschi! A sick tummy could do that.

Garrett crouched down and put two fingers on Saschi's

neck. "Did anyone call the paramedics? Saschi still has a pulse." He frowned. "Their heart is racing."

"I did," said a woman with short blond hair and a lot of tattoos. She smelled like sunshine. I recognized her as the one who led us to the table outside.

Speaking of, I wished Klaus was here with me. Together, we could hunt through the restaurant and sniff up all sorts of clues.

We learned about clues from Adam, the ghost who lives in our house, and from John, who writes books where nasty things happen to people, but things turn out okay in the end.

We also had to help Garrett when our neighbor's cat went missing. We found all sorts of clues that led us to Misty. She'd been shacking up with a man two blocks away.

He feeds me superior wet food, she said. I couldn't blame her for leaving her other cheapskate of a human behind. Naturally, Klaus and I didn't tell anyone we found her.

After Misty promised to cut us in on her treats.

Well, with Klaus tied up outside, I guessed it was up to me. I shoved my little body back out into the dining room, and started sniffing under tables, leash dragging, tail held high. I wished I could take the darn leash off. As it was, I had to be careful to not snag it on a table leg.

"Oh! Cute doggo!"

"Hey there, are you lost?"

I ignored the human voices and focused on what my nose was picking up.

Saschi had smelled like mint, it was true. Plus, soy sauce. And that old fish smell, plus what was probably their sour stomach. But there was something else... they smelled like fear. I had noticed it in the shop.

Turns out Saschi had been right to be afraid. Something was very wrong.

I just hoped they didn't die before they told us what it was.

CHAPTER 4

Garrett

I PACED the between the rows of uncomfortable blue chairs in the hospital waiting room. It smelled of antiseptic and other more noxious things. The fluorescent lights bounced off the white tiles, slowly giving me a headache.

John had taken the dogs home, while I followed the ambulance as far as the parking lot at the bottom of the hill. It went on to the top, while I parked and took the funicular up the tree lined mountain that guards the western edge of the city.

There's no parking at the teaching hospital except for emergency vehicles and some staff. Every time I've had to visit someone here, the aerial tram feels like a strange rite of passage, as if you're traversing between two worlds.

Two other people shared the waiting room with me. A woman in hijab and bright pink salwar kameez kept wiping at her red-tipped nose with a tissue. The large man next to her wore jeans and a button-down shirt, with a small black brimless cap on his head and a full beard framing his face. He would occasionally pat her hand.

I left them to their worries and sorrow, and paced the opposite end of the room, too restless to sit down.

Saschi wasn't really a friend, but I felt some responsibility toward them. I'd texted their housemate, but gotten no response so far, and the restaurant said they'd try to notify their emergency contact person.

I didn't hold out much hope. Folks like Saschi and me? We didn't have a large network of support. Those of us lucky enough to have birth family who loved and supported us were few and far between. I mean, I think things are getting better for trans and non-binary kids—at least I hope so—but for my generation, and even Saschi's? Acceptance was a hard-won thing. Too often our families wanted nothing to do with us.

It was only after I'd set up my business and been with John a few years that my family had slowly begun to realize my being trans wasn't a phase. It was who I am. Who I've always been: a boy who grew up to be a man.

Most of us have found family, forged through years of bonding over shared pain as much as shared interests. But Saschi didn't even seem to have that. Life of the party types, especially those whose major coin was gossip, didn't seem to keep many long term, close friends.

"Garrett Henson?"

The man who poked his head through door looked to be about mid-thirties. He had dark skin, the beginnings of a scruff around his face, tired eyes, and wore blue scrubs.

"That's me."

"Hi. I'm Greg, one of the ICU nurses. We usually don't let anyone into ICU except family, but Saschi specifically requested you, so I'm going to break the rules and let you back."

That's what I mean about a fragile network, and the reason I was here, pacing the fluorescent room with uncomfortable chairs.

I nodded and followed Greg through a swinging door into a long corridor with other corridors branching off. We passed the nurses' station with its computer monitors and telephones, and two women in scrubs typing furiously into computers and two others chatting quietly.

Wheelchairs littered the hall, along with a few empty gurneys.

Finally, Greg led me to the large ICU space. There were several curtained-off areas as well as two glassed-in rooms. Machines hummed, hissed, and beeped everywhere. The spiky blips of heart monitors glowed green. Nurses and doctors conferred across beds where sunken in people lay.

The place gave me the creeps. I mean, I'm no stranger to hospitals, but that doesn't mean I've ever gotten used to them. I wished I had Klaus and Marsha for company.

And I really wished John was here.

"Just up ahead," Greg said, looking over his shoulder.

I nodded again, following his footsteps as if I were Marsha and he had treats in his pocket. Come to think of it, maybe he did.

The thought made me grin, but the smile fled as quickly as it had come, because all of a sudden we stood beside Saschi's bed.

They looked thinner somehow, as if just being in the hospital had drained the spark from them. Their eyes fluttered, and they gave a soft moan.

"Garrett," they croaked.

"I'm here," I said, stepping closer. I lightly touched the

back of Saschi's hand, the one at the end of the arm not filled with tubes.

"Tell you…"

I leaned closer.

"Tell me what?"

Saschi moaned again. I looked up at Greg, but the nurse was busy checking things on the monitor next to Saschi's bed.

"Letters."

"Letters?"

The machines Saschi was attached to started beeping and whirring, then an alarm sounded. Saschi began to shake. Between trembles, they croaked out two words.

"Find out."

"Saschi! Find out what?"

A second nurse was at the bed now, pushing me aside.

"I'm sorry, sir, you're going to have to leave!"

"Saschi!"

"Now, sir!"

A third nurse was there now, all three of them crowding around Saschi, who looked so frail and small.

I backed away, leaving them to their work, then turned to find my way back to the labyrinth that would lead me to the waiting room.

Tears prickled at the back of my eyes as I moved swiftly down the hall. A flash of pink clothing stood out against white walls as someone turned the corner just ahead of me, which was a little bit strange. I didn't think most people were allowed back in this area.

I hurried on, nose filled with the scent of rubbing alcohol and illness. I hated those smells, even though surgery had brought some sense of normalcy and healing to my body.

I tried to clutch onto my mantra: "Your life at your weakest was the gateway to your strength."

Maybe those words were even true. For me, at least.

But for Saschi?

I was very afraid that the sentiment might just be too late.

CHAPTER 5

Marsha

GARRETT HAD COME HOME UPSET. He and John were sitting on the living room sofa, drinking wine and talking. Klaus and I were curled up on our big bed by the fireplace. Even though there was no fire tonight, our bed was cozy.

We had started out near Garrett, trying to comfort him, but he was too distracted, so we had decamped.

"I just don't understand what happened," Garrett said. "Saschi is so young and had seemed fine."

"Well, you're the one who thought something was off about them."

"Yeah, emotionally. I didn't think there was something physically wrong with them."

"Did you find any clues?" Klaus asked me for the millionth time.

"I told you I didn't. Not in the restaurant, at least. Saschi smelled like mint gum. Old fish. And they smelled kind of sour. And afraid."

"Hmph." Klaus put his nose between his paws and

closed his eyes. *"That is a strange combination of smells. And except for the mint, it doesn't sound like Saschi at all."*

Klaus was right, but I wasn't sure what the strange smells could mean.

I saw movement at the top of the big, wide, wood staircase. It had a nice carpet for our claws to grip—which was a good thing, because our little legs didn't do so well on stairs—and was carved in fancy, squared-off shapes that Garrett always said "reflected the true Craftsman heritage of the home."

He talks funny that way. I just accept it, even though John sometimes laughs at him and says "Babe." As if that means something.

Humans. Sometimes understanding them is really hard.

The movement resolved itself into Adam, one hand on the wood railing, coming down the stairs. He was slightly less than solid, which meant I could see the framed photos on the staircase wall through his torso and head.

It's pretty weird, but another thing I've come to accept. Adam wore the only clothes he had: leather pants, big leather boots, a leather vest over a naked, hairy, muscular chest, and a leather hat with a small brim. He also wore a heavy chain around his neck. Not like a dog collar chain, but some kind of decoration. Some humans like decoration. Others? Not so much.

I don't mind a little bling on my collar, but I'm naturally beautiful enough without much extra sparkle.

The ghost's face lit in a smile when he saw me watching him. The smile lifted the big furry mustache on his upper lip and made his eyes crinkle, which I liked.

Eyes crinkling is the human equivalent of wagging your tail. Or, for corgis who lost their tails, your butt.

When Klaus is happy enough, he wiggles both his tail and his butt. He just can't help it.

I gave a soft woof at the ghost. Klaus snorted and jerked, opening his eyes.

"What are you barking at, Marsha?" John asked.

I didn't bother to reply. I just got up and threaded my way past the big comfy chairs, over the rug, past the coffee table and sofa, heading to the stairs.

"Do you think it's the ghost again?" Garrett asked, voice hushed as if my excellent corgi ears couldn't hear him.

"Who knows, with those two? But that reminds me, I want to do more research about Adam this week. Make some time to go through that box of memorabilia Klaus and Marsha found."

Klaus had discovered a hidden door in the back of the big closet in Garrett and John's bedroom. The closet we were "under no circumstances to enter. Do you hear me?"

Is it my fault that leather shoes are so tasty and satis-fying to chew on?

At any rate, that's when we found Adam. There was a box of his things stuffed into the corgi-sized, angled room. I guess this had been his house when he was alive.

"The Portland LGBT Archives might have something, if the internet doesn't," Garrett was saying.

Adam looked at the two men.

::I guess they're talking about me again.::

Adam's voice sounded inside my mind. I'm still getting used to that. It's a little strange.

I gave a soft woof as a yes.

::It's good that John wants to do some research. There's a lot in the box, but I have so many more stories I could tell, if only...::

The ghost stared off in the distance until I nudged his big boot with my nose and yelped. I keep forgetting how cold Adam is. And that my nose goes through his boot, instead of bumping against it.

"Marsha?" Garrett asked from the couch. "What's the matter, girl?"

"She probably wants more food. That one is always ready to eat."

And why do you think my coat is so glossy and beautiful, hmm? It doesn't get this way from not eating.

"A snack is a good idea," Klaus said, finally getting up to join me.

We both trotted to the kitchen to see if there was any kibble left in our bowls. Adam followed us.

He's always interested in what we're doing. I guess after not talking to anyone for a long time, the fact that we can see and hear him must be nice.

Adam leaned against the deep green kitchen cabinets, tracing a finger across the white countertops while Klaus and I went straight to the narrow wood table in the middle of the kitchen. The table had a low shelf where our food and water bowls rested in circles cut out of the wood. They were just the right height for both of us.

Drat. No kibble. Who had eaten it all?

Klaus shrugged and lapped at the water dish, while I nosed around, seeking out stray nuggets of crunchy goodness.

::*Who was this waiter who died?*:: Adam asked. He must have been listening for a while before coming downstairs. He does that sometimes.

"Saschi," I said, continuing my hunt. Garrett and John were too darn clean! *"Garrett and John both liked them, and they were always nice to us."*

"But John also said they were a terrible gossip." Klaus softly barked.

::*Hmmm,*:: Adam said, stroking the edges of that huge mustache. ::*I know that gossip is currency in the gay community, but not everyone likes it.*::

"What do you mean?" Klaus asked.

::*Gossip can get you into trouble. People don't like their secrets revealed.*::

That made sense. I didn't like it when John found my secret stashes of toys or treats. He always scolded me for it, which I just don't understand. I mean, John has things he keeps stored away, and so does Garrett. Why can't I?

"Do you think someone deliberately hurt Saschi?" Klaus asked.

I stopped my little paws on the wood kitchen floor and lifted my nose from the final—clean—corner.

"You mean, someone might want Saschi dead?" The thought made my tummy quiver.

We both looked up at Adam. The ghost is very tall in his boots. The pendant light above the sink glowed through his face, but I could still see that his expression was worried.

::*I'm afraid it's likely. You may want to get your dads to return to the scene of the crime.*::

Klaus and I looked at each other.

"How are we going to do that?" Klaus asked.

"We'll figure out a way," I said. *"I'm going back to lie down and ponder it."*

Ponder was the right word. I'd learned it from John. It means to think about something carefully.

And we were going to need to think very carefully about this, indeed.

CHAPTER 6
Garrett

IT WAS FRIDAY MORNING, and John and I decided to take the dogs out and pick up coffee and treats before I opened the shop. My shop, Dandy Lion's Design and Décor, took healthy amounts of patience, perseverance, and a certain amount of magic to remain in the black. I didn't have Glinda the Good Witch to help me out, so coffee would have to do.

We wandered down the street beneath flowering cherry trees as Marsha and Klaus tugged at their leashes, snapping at the falling blossoms, then stopping to sniff random bushes or fence posts, a thing a friend of mine used to call "checking their pee-mail."

We walked the three blocks to Pride Street, heading toward our favorite café, Bruiser's Best Beans. The smell of roasting coffee wafted toward us on the spring breeze.

Marsha tugged harder on her leash, practically cutting off circulation in my hand. Every time she jerked, the leather bag slung across my chest bumped my hip. Hard.

"Klaus, calm down!" John said. He was having the same issue.

"As soon as they smell the coffee," I said, "they know treats are in store. Plus, I think Klaus has a crush on Bruiser."

Bruiser was an English bulldog with a severe breathing problem. He co-owned the café with our favorite lesbian couple, Bex and Jacki.

John snorted back a laugh. "I don't know, Marsha might give Klaus a run for his money where Bruiser is concerned."

John was right. All three dogs seemed to have major canine crushes on each other. As soon as we turned onto Pride, Marsha barked happily and Bruiser leapt up from where he'd been snoozing in the sun in front of the open café door and wagged his tawny rump excitedly, tongue lolling out of his open mouth. His coloring was the same as Klaus's, golden tan and white, but other than that, and four legs, the dogs couldn't look less alike.

Marsha yanked the leash again and I gave in, quickening my steps. Her tail was going triple time. So was Klaus's. Bruiser trotted toward us, the barrel of his body rolling over sturdy legs. If a smashed-in face like his could be said to grin, he was definitely doing it.

The dogs all circled around each other in joyous excitement, happily sniffing one another in greeting.

"Okay, you three," John finally said, "let's get you tethered outside the café. Daddy needs some coffee."

"And a breakfast sandwich." I was getting hungry and needed sustenance before a day of helping antiques shoppers. Plus, I had a new client coming in just after opening, and I needed to be at my best and brightest. I couldn't do that without food and caffeine.

We made short work of getting the dogs settled, their leashes looped around handy eye bolts and fresh water in the dishes that were always outside in sunny weather.

Entering the bright café, the coffee smell only intensified, mingling with scents of cinnamon muffins and eggy-cheesy panini grilling in the sandwich press.

The place was a cozy haven filled with blond wood benches and tables. Plants graced the edges of the front windows and perched on the tall bookcases that held coffee and tea accoutrement for sale. A couple of comfy stuffed chairs crouched near the back corner, both occupied by people reading books and drinking coffee or tea.

Bex smiled from behind the register, her short blond hair adorably tousled as usual, green eyes snapping from behind chunky, blue-framed glasses. She wore a white T-shirt topped with a striped vest.

"Nice vest!" I said, approaching the counter.

"Back atcha," she replied, gesturing to my vintage paisley waistcoat.

Jacki waved from her station at the espresso machine. Her short, coiled hair was framed by a brilliant orange scarf that complemented her dark skin and yellow tee.

Bex took our order and then rung us up.

As John stuffed some bills in the tip jar, her sunny face sobered.

"Wait a minute," she said. "You were at the restaurant yesterday, weren't you?"

I froze, hand hovering over the treat bowl that held little heart shaped dog cookies.

"It's so terrible, what happened to Saschi," she went on talking. "Do you think they'll be okay?"

Next to me, John shrugged and shook his head.

"We haven't heard yet," I said. "I went to the hospital afterwards, but they were in pretty bad shape."

I grabbed a cookie for each dog, then had a thought.

"Do you know any if Saschi had any family?"

It was my understanding that they didn't really. At least, that was the impression the hospital gave.

Bex shook her head. "I don't know. I didn't know them that well, but frankly, I'm not surprised this happened."

John's head snapped up sharply. "What do you mean?"

Bex looked at the two of us, her pale eyebrows arched in surprise.

"You know. They were always gossiping. I wouldn't be surprised if someone got upset and finally took matters into their own hands."

"Wait," I said, "you think this is murder?"

"Attempted," John said. "Sachi's still alive. Let's not get ahead of ourselves."

"I don't understand," I said. "Saschi is so vibrant and fun. And they were always so nice to us."

"Yeah," Jacki said, wiping her hands on a dish towel. "Saschi was real nice. Unless you were the one they were gossiping about. Saschi said some terrible things, you know?"

"Yeah, but doesn't everyone?" I asked. "I mean, this community runs on gossip…"

Bex's brow furrowed. "Not the kind Saschi dished out."

A line began to form behind us, and it was clear the conversation was over, at least for the moment.

John and I huddled around the condiment station, doctoring our coffee with sugar and coconut creamer. He looked as troubled as I felt.

"I don't understand how this could happen," I began.

"Let's wait 'til we're outside."

I nodded. I stuffed the dog cookies in my right pocket, and we grabbed our cups and headed outside where the three doggos happily rested beneath a table, half in sun and half in the shade of a maple tree. I plopped down on a wooden bench behind one of the two-top picnic tables, slung my bag off my shoulder, then reached under the table to give a cookie to each waiting fur face. The two corgis gently took their cookies in their teeth as if they were the Crown Jewels, while Bruiser slobbered all over my hand, trying to get to his.

I grimaced and dug a wet wipe from my bag as John squeezed in next to me. He nudged the dogs with his toe to make room for his legs. Bruiser grunted but shifted his bulk, while Klaus and Marsha looked up at me happily panting as if awaiting another treat.

"One cookie is all you get," I said to them. I swear, they sighed in disappointment, then settled their noses back down on their paws. Cute as buttons, those two. Bruiser began snoring. Or maybe he was just breathing, it was hard to tell. With bulldogs, it was kind of all the same.

I sipped my milky brew, staring at the green leaves emerging on the maple tree.

"I really need to get back to the hospital and see how Saschi's doing."

John nodded, sipping his own coffee, but his eyes looked distant, as if he was thinking a million things. I was used to that, living with a writer. Their heads were often elsewhere. But right now? I knew he wasn't thinking of a plot to one of his books. He was thinking about what had happened in our own community.

"Brings it close to home, doesn't it?" he said, giving voice to his thoughts.

I nodded. "Sure does."

Bex dropped our breakfast sandwiches off. We gave our thanks, and she turned to head back to the customers inside.

She stopped and turned at the door. "You know, I didn't mean anything by what I said, and neither did Jacki. About someone killing them. You know we both liked Saschi, right?"

I nodded.

"But if you find out anything," she said, "you'll let us know?"

"I will."

Then, with the barest flicker of a smile, she headed back inside.

I looked down at the cheesy-eggy panini that I'd been so hungry for just fifteen minutes before. Now I wasn't even sure I could eat at all.

I shoved the sandwich away and took a gulp of my coffee.

"You have to eat, babe. You can't work in the shop all day with no food. You also can't spend all your time worrying about Saschi. Don't you have a client this morning?"

I gave John's hand a squeeze. He was right. Life had to go one. Otherwise, what was the point?

I picked up my sandwich and took a bite, but barely tasted anything. I couldn't stop thinking of Saschi lying on the restaurant floor, and then what they said to me in the hospital.

Find out.

Find out what? Maybe Bex and Jacki were right to suspect foul play. Saschi had also mentioned letters. But who even wrote letters anymore?

"It still doesn't make any sense," I mused.

"Babe. You're gonna have to let this one go."

"You're probably right." But I didn't like it. Why would someone as seemingly healthy as Saschi end up in the ICU?

John bit into his sandwich, and I took another tentative bite from mine. It tasted like sand.

The day, it was beautiful. The sun was shining, but I felt cold inside. I couldn't stop thinking about Saschi, and what had happened, and who might have wanted them dead.

And why.

CHAPTER 7
Marsha

JOHN AND GARRETT were getting ready to go. They shifted around on their bench, making those "I'm done with my sandwich"—but didn't give the dogs one bite!—and "will you get the trash?" noises.

But I'd half listened to their earlier conversation, about Saschi being attempted-murdered. I could have told them that. Something was very off about the waiter's collapse to the ground. My nose hadn't picked up on much, but that didn't mean I hadn't missed something.

Much as I hated to admit it, Klaus was a better sniffer than I am. Which gave me an idea…

"Klaus!"

"What?"

"We have to convince them to walk by the sushi restaurant!"

Bruiser snorted, not that it meant anything. Bruiser just can't help it. He's a bulldog. They snort.

"Why?" Klaus asked.

John was untying our leashes from the tether. We needed to work fast.

"I need you to sniff around. See if you can find something I missed."

"But the restaurant will be closed," Bruiser said.

I looked at his smashed-in face. Dang. He was right. But there was a tugging in my tummy that told me I needed to follow my corgi instincts.

And my corgi instincts told me we had to return to the scene of the crime.

"Saschi worked the tables outside. Maybe something happened to them there!"

"Ready, puppers?" Garrett asked.

"Bruiser, you distract them. Klaus, get ready to run."

We all stood up.

"Now!" I barked.

Bruiser shoved his barrel of a body into Garrett's legs.

"Aww! You want a head scratch, big fella?" Garrett dropped our leashes and bent to give Bruiser some attention.

Klaus and I grabbed our leashes in our mouths and took off running down the street just as John exited the café.

He began yelling and gave chase.

We were faster.

"Go, Klaus, go!"

"I'm going!"

Corgis are super fast, and trained to run through obstacles, herding cattle or sheep. Even the shoppers on Pride Street were no match for me and Klaus. John's legs are a lot longer than ours, and he's pretty fit, so he finally caught up to me and grabbed for my leash. I bit down harder on the tasty leather and dodged away from his grasping hands.

"Dang it! Marsha P. Johnson, you get back here!"

I put on another burst of speed. Klaus was ahead now, racing toward the sushi place. I followed his little white butt and flag of a tail down the sidewalk, dodging a stroller and several legs and feet. Why were so many people out walking this morning? Shouldn't they all be at work?

Finally, I reached the restaurant. John was just behind me. Times like this, I really wished he didn't go running so often. It would've been better if Garrett had chased us down. He's a lot slower.

"Got you, you rascal! What are you up to? It isn't like you two to pull a runner."

Klaus was sniffing the edges of the outdoor front patio, along the edges of the building. I licked John to distract him, buying Klaus more time.

"Don't think being cute is getting you off the hook, Marsha."

"What's happening?" Garrett walked up. "Why did they run like that?"

"Heck if I know," John said. "You want to get Klaus? I don't dare let go of this one."

"Klaus! Did you find anything?"

"Not yet," he woofed back. *"But I think there's something in the planter box."*

Near the front entrance were two low wood boxes planted with some kind of green bushes. They formed a sort of corridor leading to the big front door.

I jerked in John's arms.

"No, you don't!"

"Klaus, what are you up to?" Garrett asked, reaching for my friend.

I barked and jerked toward the planter box again, hoping John would figure it out.

Klaus barked at Garrett and backed away from his hands.

I barked and barked and barked.

"Look in the planter boxes!"

"The planter boxes!" Klaus echoed.

A face appeared in the glass top of the front doors. Daniel. The owner scowled at us. I growled back and he disappeared again.

"I think they want something," Garrett said, his pale brow furrowing, the way it did when he was puzzled about something.

"Planter boxes!" I barked again.

Klaus propped his front paws on the edge of one of the boxes and started sniffing around.

He gave a short bark. *"Something's here!"*

"What did you find?" Garrett asked, leaning over the box.

John carried me over to investigate.

"Do you see anything?"

"Klaus, if you move, I could look at what you're trying to show me," Garrett said.

Klaus scooched over, front paws still balanced on the planter box, his little back legs carrying him to the side.

Garrett looked, then reached under the bushes, feeling around in the dirt.

"What's this?"

"You see something?" John asked, leaning closer. I stretched as far as I could from my perch in his arms, trying to see past the back of Garrett's head.

Klaus looked up at me and barked.

"I found something! Just like you said!"

Garrett whipped a handkerchief from his trouser pocket and pulled something out from under the green leaves of the bush, holding it carefully in the white square of cloth.

He held it up to the morning sun.

"What is it?" John asked.

"Not sure. But I think it's one of those nicotine refills for a vape pen."

John grabbed my leash in one hand and set me down. I trotted to Klaus who had all four fuzzy feet firmly back on the patio.

"Good job," I said.

He puffed his little tan and white chest out, looking quite pleased with himself.

"Thank you," he said.

"You think that's what happened to them? Someone dosed Saschi with nicotine?"

"I don't know," Garrett replied, slipping the object into his pocket. He checked his watch and swore softly. "I have to open the store. But we're going to find out what happened to Saschi if it kills me."

John pulled him in for a hug, Klaus and I parked at their legs. John was taller than Garrett, the way I'm taller than Klaus. I gave Klaus's snoot a lick.

"What's that for?" he asked.

"You did a good job today."

"We both did," he said. *"You're the one who came up with the plan."*

The four of us began the walk to Garrett's store, which was just around the corner from Bruiser's café. The sushi restaurant had been a definite detour. But worth it.

"Do you need me to go to the hospital today?" John asked as we walked.

"Maybe we could go after work? I know you have a lot of writing on deck, and I don't want to interrupt that. Besides, I need to think about this whole situation some more."

We rounded the corner, and the person with rainbow shoes was standing there, looking heartbroken. Their cropped yellow hair and smooth dark skin were the same, but there was no green heart on their shirt today. They were head to toe in black, except for the rainbow shoes.

As soon as they saw us, they burst into tears.

John and Garrett rushed forward, Klaus and I leading the way.

"Oh, my goodness!" Garrett clucked like an old hen. "What's wrong?"

"Saschi..." the rainbow shoe person gulped out.

I parked my butt and looked up, waiting for them to finish their sentence.

"Saschi is dead!"

CHAPTER 8

Garrett

I SWEAR, my heart stopped in my chest. One hand clenched Klaus's leash, the other reached for John's hand. His cool skin immediately slipped into my slightly sweaty palm, squeezing my fingers for reassurance.

"Let's all go inside," I said.

I unlocked the door, but kept the sign flipped to closed.

"John," I asked. "Can you go in the back and make us all a cup of tea?"

"Sure," said my handsome partner. He unclipped both dogs' leashes, hung them on the hook behind the counter, and loped off toward the burgundy velvet curtain that partitioned off my WC, break room, and shipping area from the main part of the store.

Both dogs sniffed around the person's legs. I cursed myself, trying to recall what name they'd introduced themselves with the last time they were in the shop.

As a store owner, that was a thing I tried hard to practice, but still wasn't very good at.

"Let's go to Art Deco and sit."

They nodded, face still streaked with tears. Klaus and Marsha trotted through the store, weaving between old sideboards, dressers, and chairs, nails alternately clicking on hardwood, then muffled on the variety of rugs strewn about. All for sale, of course.

I ran a finger over a statue of a dancing woman. I needed to make time to dust in the afternoon. But first, I had to get through this, and my client meeting.

Yikes! My client was supposed to show up in thirty minutes.

"Have a seat. Please." I gestured to two overstuffed, deco style club chairs covered in a rich, marigold colored velvet.

The person plopped their skinny body down and hunched over themselves.

"What's your name again?" I asked gently. "I'm sorry I don't remember from last time. My name is Garrett. My pronouns are he/him."

"I'm Yarrow. They/them."

Just like Saschi.

"How long were you friends with Saschi, Yarrow?" Yarrow was a good name for them. Their tightly coiled, short hair was dyed the color of golden yarrow flowers.

Yarrow nodded, scrubbing a hand over their cheeks. I reached for the clean handkerchief in my pocket, then realized I'd wrapped the nicotine vial in it. Dang.

"I'll be right back."

I rushed to the front counter for a tissue box. When I returned, John was there, setting a tea tray on a vintage black and silver coffee table. Classic Deco.

"Thank you, sweetie," I said, sitting back down in my

chair. John took a spot on a blue velvet love seat across from the matching chairs.

"Yarrow? This is my partner, John. And you've already met Klaus and Marsha."

That got half a smile, at least. I noticed both dogs had lain down on the carpet, one on either side of Yarrow's legs, flanking the distressed person like two little library lions.

John leaned forward and poured the tea from a white China pot into flowered cups.

"Coconut creamer? Sugar?"

Yarrow nodded, so John added a bit of both, doing the same for mine. He drank his tea black, the way it was meant to be drunk, he always said.

By the time we were settled and sipping, Yarrow seemed to have calmed down. They gazed out the big front windows toward the maple trees that lined my little street and sighed.

"I went to visit Saschi last night. They were asking for me. The nurses said no family had come forward, so they were letting in anyone Saschi asked for."

Yarrow gripped the teacup so hard, I was afraid they might crack the China.

"So, Saschi had no family?" John's voice was gentle.

Marsha nuzzled Yarrow's black jeans. Yarrow reached down with one hand and patted Marsha's head.

"Not that they ever spoke to. I was going to ask around today and see if anyone else knew who to contact."

"When did Saschi pass?" I asked. Yarrow's eyes welled up with tears again, and I felt like a real jerk. But if I was going to find who did this to Saschi, I had to start asking questions.

Yarrow set down the teacup on the tray and grabbed another tissue, blowing their nose loudly, and dabbing at their red rimmed eyes.

"I got a call this morning. Just half an hour ago. I… I didn't know where else to go. Someone said you were there? At the restaurant?"

Yarrow turned those dark sad eyes my way. Klaus scooted forward and put both his paws on Yarrow's rainbow shoes. Animals are so good at giving comfort.

"We were. We were eating dinner when Saschi fell."

"Did you see anything?"

I looked at John, as if he could help. What could we tell this person? They were already so upset. It was never an easy thing to tell someone their friend may have been murdered.

"Look," Yarrow said. Their voice turned sharp. "No one is going to help Saschi. No one except a handful of us even care. If you were there, you have to help me!"

"Help you with what?" John asked.

"Help me find who killed them!"

Now it was my turn to lean forward. I stared into Yarrow's eyes. They didn't hesitate, but stared right back, a fire glimmering behind the tears. They might be bubbly, and skinny, and bright as spring most of the time, but I could see they had a fierce side. And that just might be what we needed to figure all of this out.

But I needed to tread carefully. After all, I didn't know Yarrow. Maybe they had killed Saschi and regretted it now. Or maybe it really had been an accident.

But the nicotine vial dug into my thigh, and my gut told me this was no accident.

"Let's start at the beginning," I said. "What makes you

think Saschi was murdered? And who would want them dead?"

Yarrow sat back in their chair, relaxing slightly, now that they knew we were taking them seriously.

"Saschi was… a lot. I mean, I loved them. I really did. They were fun, and funny, and a good friend to me when I needed someone. But Saschi also loved to gossip."

John and I both nodded. That, we knew too well.

"And sometimes, they grew mean. I would always ask if it was that time of the month, you know, joking about the hormones they were taking. But I think they had bad patches. Saschi would get really dark sometimes, and that's when the viciousness came out. They hurt a lot of people when they were in those states."

I knew all about mood swings from hormones, though mine had evened out. In the beginning though? Second adolescence is a doozy.

John crossed his foot over his knee, tapping his burgundy Keds with one long finger. "And you think one of those people may have wanted Saschi dead?"

Yarrow shrugged and took a sip of tea. "I'm not sure about that. But healthy people don't just fall to the floor and die within days!"

"This is a hard question," I said, "but if we're going to help you, there are going to be a lot more questions like this."

Yarrow sat up tall, squared their shoulders, and lifted their chin. "Ask me anything. I've got nothing to hide."

Everyone has something to hide, I thought.

"Did Saschi do drugs?"

"That's your question?" Yarrow gave a sharp laugh. "In this community? There are drugs everywhere. But no.

Not really. I mean, Saschi sometimes drank too much—when they were in their moods, like I said—but other than that? I never saw them take anything. Not even at big parties when folks were cutting loose."

"Did Saschi smoke?" John asked.

"Like regular cigarettes? No. They used to but quit quit some time ago. I was happy when they quit." Yarrow shuddered, as if the very thought was anathema. It's funny what lines we draw, isn't it? "They did chew nicotine gum, though. But I think they were tapering off."

If Saschi chewed nicotine gum, that meant they didn't vape. So where did the vial come from?

"Why do you ask?" Yarrow said, furrowing their otherwise smooth brow.

I re-crossed my legs, stalling. Yarrow may have been Saschi's friend, but I still didn't know them well enough to trust them with all the information.

"Someone dropped a nicotine vial," John said, quickly covering the awkward silence. "And we weren't sure if it was Saschi's."

I sent him a look of thanks, then set down my teacup.

"Okay," I said. Sliding my phone from my rear pocket, I opened a notes app. "Who's on your top ten list here? Who might have wanted Saschi dead?"

CHAPTER 9

Marsha

"ADAM!" I called, staring at the double doors leading to the Forbidden Closet.

"What are you doing?" Klaus asked. Garrett and John were eating dinner downstairs, and I figured this would be a good time to ask the ghost some questions.

"What does it look like?" I asked. *"I want to talk to the ghost."*

Klaus plopped down beside me and started cleaning in between his toes.

"Can't you do that later? Ugh."

Klaus ignored me, and kept on loudly licking and biting, cleaning his feet as if there weren't more important things to do right now.

"Adam!"

The ghost slid through one of the wood doors, almost bumping into my nose with those big boots of his.

Startled, I yelped and jumped back. I like Adam, but yeah, I'm not really used to touching him yet. It's weird. And cold.

"Neat!" Klaus said. *"You didn't open the doors this time!"*

::I've been practicing moving through physical objects,:: Adam said inside my head. *::It's a little disorienting, but much easier than trying to actually move things.::*

Adam could move small, light things sometimes, or do things like open doors, but I could tell it cost him effort. I wished I could move through doors like that. It meant the closet would never be off limits.

Think of all the shoes I would have access to, whenever I wanted them.

I must have drifted off, thinking of shoes, because the next thing I knew, Adam was snapping a ghost finger in front of my nose and Klaus was nudging my side with his big wet nose.

"Sorry!" I said.

Adam crossed the bedroom to sit on the window seat and look out onto the back yard. Klaus and I propped our paws on the bench, looking through the open curtains, trying to see what the ghost was looking at. It was dark. All I could see were the little lights glowing in some of the garden beds.

::What did you want me for?:: Adam said. *::Not that I ever mind company.::*

He sounded a little lonely. We needed to get him a ghost dog or something, but I had no idea how to do that.

"We think someone was murdered," Klaus said. He sounded a bit too happy about it.

"Klaus!" I barked. *"That isn't something to enjoy!"*

Well, unless they were a Very Bad Person, maybe. I certainly sometimes wanted to bite Very Bad People myself. And humans can be a lot more violent than dogs.

Adam twisted the ends of his big mustache, looking

thoughtful. Humans always did something when they were thinking hard. Guess it didn't matter if they were alive or dead. Still human. Still the same.

::What makes you think someone killed this person?::

"Well," I said, getting all four paws on the patterned rug again. I don't like standing on my hind legs for long. I'd much rather be comfy. *"They seemed fine, then fell down suddenly. Garrett went to see them in the hospital, and it didn't sound good."*

"Then a person came to Garrett's store this morning and said Saschi was dead!" Klaus barked.

::Saschi? That's the person's name?::

I nodded. Adam was looking at us attentively now.

"And that's not all!" I said. *"I led us in a jail break today! We got away from John and Garrett and went back to the Scene of the Crime!"*

"And I found a clue!"

"A clue! A clue!"

There were footsteps in the hall. Uh oh.

John poked his head into the room.

"What's going on in here, you two?"

"The ghost!" Klaus said. *"We're talking with the ghost!"*

I looked from Adam, to John, and back again. Humans are so dense sometimes. We had told John and Garrett about Adam, but they still didn't quite get it, even after looking through some boxes of his stuff.

John's face cleared. "Oh! Is it the ghost again?"

He stepped tentatively into the room, brown eyes sweeping over the window seat. Adam fluttered one of the curtains. John's eyes grew wide.

"Adam? Is that you?"

Adam chuckled, and moved the curtain again. *::It is.::*

John shook his head. He couldn't hear Adam the way we could, I guess.

"Well, okay then. Nice to not see you again Adam." Then he looked at us and said in his stern voice, "You two, behave yourselves, okay? And try to keep it down. I'm working."

John worked at night sometimes, but Garrett complained that he shouldn't. So how were we supposed to know? I just panted at him and smiled. He stood there for a moment, running a hand through his short, almost black hair, then turned and left.

"*So,*" I said. "*Where were we?*"

::*You found a clue,*:: Adam prompted.

"*Yes!*" Klaus woofed, trying to keep his voice soft. We didn't want John or Garrett back up here. Not yet at least. "*I found a thing! And Garrett wrapped it in a handkerchief and put it in his pocket!*"

Adam's eyes focused with interest. ::*What was thing you found, Klaus?*::

"*I'm not sure. It was small and plastic. Clear at the bottom with a black part on top. It didn't taste very good.*"

Adam looked at me for more information. Of course, he did. I was clearly the smarter dog in this situation.

"*Garrett and John said it was a vial of nicotine.*"

The ghost's eyebrows raised so high I could barely see them beneath his leather cap.

::*Why would anyone need a vial of nicotine? Why not just smoke cigarettes? And where would a person even get such a thing?*::

Klaus and I looked at each other, confused. Why did humans do anything?

Meanwhile, Adam muttered to himself about didn't

people just take party drugs anymore or something. I couldn't quite tell what he was on about.

Finally, I gave a small bark, not enough to alert Garrett and John, but enough that Adam stopped his muttering and sighed.

::Okay. Sorry about that. Everything's just a bit confusing since you all brought me into this,:: —he waved a hand in a circle—, *::era. Things were different in the '80s.::*

He stared out at the darkness again. *::Very different.::*

The look on his face was so wistful, it made me wonder if ghosts saw ghosts of their own. Because it certainly looked as if he was seeing people.

Adam must have realized his mind was wandering because he smacked the palms of his hands on his leather jeans and peered down at us again.

::Tell me about this Saschi. What kind of person was she? He?::

"They!" we barked.

He nodded, as if that made sense. *::They. Yeah. That's a better way to describe half the people I knew back in the day, isn't it? Tell me about them.::*

"Weeelll," Klaus began. *"Saschi wore bright shoes. And makeup. But wore regular pants and shirts."*

"And they were always nice to us," I added. *"Garrett and John liked them, too. But I guess Saschi made a lot of other people mad."*

There was that keen gaze again.

::Mad, how?::

"Saschi liked to gossip," Klaus said.

Adam stroked his luxuriant mustache again. *::The gay community always did run on gossip. All small communities* *and subcultures do. But not everyone wants their secrets told, do they?::*

Klaus and I just looked at each other again. I think we were both remembering the time we found a hole in the back of the kitchen pantry and started hiding treats there.

That led to a rat problem. Luckily, John and Garrett blamed the rats for the treat stealing. Mostly. John did look suspicious that they were our favorites, and that no other food had made it into the hole before the rat arrived.

"Secrets can get people into trouble," I said. And draw rats into your home.

Adam leaned over and scratched my head. His fingers were icy cold and not firm enough to actually scratch. It just felt weird, and I wished he would stop. Luckily, he sat back before I had to bark at him. I'd rather not hurt his feelings.

::Secrets can get people into a lot of trouble,:: he agreed. *::And if they're bad enough, sometimes they can get people killed.::*

"Killed!" Klaus barked. Why he was so startled, I don't know. Garrett and John already thought that was a *possibility.*

::Killed,:: Adam repeated. *::Especially if there's blackmail involved. You have to find a way to tell your humans that.::*

It was a very good idea. But I had no idea how we were going to do it.

CHAPTER 10

Adam

IT WAS STRANGE, being back. I'd been in limbo for so long, kind of a strange, half sleep. Until the cute little dogs figured out a way into the back closet and started digging through my boxes, I was barely aware that time had moved on.

The rascals made me miss my own dog, Lucy. I wondered where she had gone. When I went into hospice care, my household said they would take care of her. I hope she lived a long and happy life after I was gone.

I also wondered if the disease that took me and so many of my friends was still around. It had to be, right?

I paced the halls of the old Craftsman house I used to share with three other men. Many people my age had been kicked out of our families, so we formed new families of our own. We took care of each other, and we fought with each other.

But after the petty bickering, at the end of the day, we also fought side by side. We fought the government who did not care about us. We fought the cops who beat and humiliated us.

We fought to live.

I wondered what people were fighting for now? No one read newspapers anymore, it seemed. I hadn't seen any around the house. There were just unfamiliar electronics on side tables, and people always staring at metal objects that looked like tiny televisions, or super compact computers. Not the clunky massive things that were just barely available by the time I died.

It looked like a lot of things had changed. But the gay gossip mill? Jealousy? Hatred, even?

Looked like all of that was alive and well.

As the French used to say: The more things change, the more they stay the same.

CHAPTER 11

Garrett

I STOOD behind the front counter of the shop, a long-cold cup of coffee at my elbow. The counter was a long, polished hardwood sideboard that I had raised onto a dais, so it was tall enough to create a border between me and clients, making it clear this was not another piece of furniture for sale.

The computer was open to my design board. I was re-doing a living room for the head of a local start-up who had made a lot of money a decade ago and now mostly coasted, pretending to work by pumping small amounts of money into other people's projects, while taking a title and share of the profits for his role in the company.

In a different time and different strata of society, I guess Tim would have been a "lady who lunched."

Regardless, I'd been poking at the design for an hour without getting anywhere. The mood board still had the same old images and color swatches, just rearranged.

The call had come that morning. Someone had found Saschi's birth family, but they wanted nothing to do with

Saschi. Not while Saschi was alive, and certainly not now that they were dead.

I had offered to organize a small fundraiser to pay for cremation and Saschi's friend Yarrow would head up the memorial. Where that would be held, and when, we didn't yet know. Frankly, I didn't trust that Yarrow could hold themself together long enough to make it happen. If that was the case, John and Bex said they would step in to help.

"Garrett!" A bark came from the back of the store.

"What are you barking at, Marsha P.?" I called back.

The dogs were behind the velvet curtain that cordoned off the shop from the back rooms. I heard scrabbling. Digging. Uh oh.

With a glance at the shop door—I'd had zero customers in the last hour—I headed toward the sweep of burgundy velvet and stepped on through.

"Garrett!" Argh.

"What? You had better not be making a mess in my stock room! How many times have I told you?"

I stomped back as hard as my leather brogues would allow and stopped in the open doorway of the storeroom where I kept items that needed pricing and had a long shipping table where I packaged smaller objects to mail.

Klaus and Marsha were under that table, ripping at a box. One of Saschi's boxes.

Great. Just great. "You two better not be chewing up what's in those boxes!"

I had agreed to store the few pitiful remnants of Saschi's life until we figured out what the family wanted. Now that we knew, I was going to suggest to Yarrow that any sentimental items be passed out to friends at the memorial.

That is, if Saschi had many friends. I was beginning to wonder.

Marsha had an envelope held delicately between her teeth. It was black, like the kind that held a card or invitation.

Klaus's head was deep inside the box. I could hear him rooting around.

"Klaus!" I slapped my hands. His head jerked up, his butt scooted backwards, tail out, and he crashed into Marsha, who yelped and dropped the envelope.

"You two. I swear. You know you're supposed to be on your best behavior in the store! And those are Saschi's boxes! If you damaged anything…" I let the threat die, because I knew I could never punish Klaus and Marsha too badly.

Unfortunately for me, they knew it, too.

Marsha placed a paw on the black envelope and slid it toward me.

"What is that?"

I reached for it, picking it up carefully. There were tiny indentations in the rich black paper from her teeth, but Marsha really had been careful with it. Nothing was ripped or torn.

The back flap was open and looked if it had never been sealed.

When I pulled the paper out and opened it, my blood ran cold. The note was handwritten, and unfinished. But what I could make out did not look good at all.

"I know what you did, and who you did it with. Some people aren't going to like that very much, are they? If you value your reputation, leave me the biggest tip of your life.

In cash.

Put it in this envelope and slip it into my apron Wednesday evening. I'll be waiting for you."

I hurried to the boxes, gently shooing Klaus and Marsha away. Crouching beneath the table, I pulled out the box Klaus had been digging in, scooted it out, then plopped myself onto the wood floor.

Before I looked inside, I cocked my head, listening. The shop was still silent. All I could hear was the mild murmur of traffic outside. A couple of laughing voices and some birdsong.

Good. No customers.

Pulling back the flaps of cardboard, I peered inside. There were trinkets and mementos scattered across the top, with what had probably been neat stacks of paper beneath, until the dogs had gotten to the box. And with the disturbed papers?

Was an open packet of black envelopes, just like the one in my hand. But stuck to one side was another note, in big block letters. It looked nothing like the note in the black envelope, even though some of the words were the same.

I know what you did, too. Better watch out.

"Oh, Saschi. What have you done?"

"Blackmail! Adam said there might be blackmail!"

It looked as if at least one of the people Saschi had been blackmailing had threatened to turn the tables.

Marsha barked again.

"Marsha, not now. I need a minute, okay?"

Marsha whuffed softly but didn't say any more.

Whipping out my phone, I sent a quick text to John.

I think the dogs have found something. It's about Saschi. Text me back or come by if you get a break.

John went into "do not disturb" mode when he was writing, but I knew he would check the phone on his next break. We'd had to institute that rule in case of emergencies, because otherwise he wouldn't check his messages for hours.

What can I say? He was weird, but I loved him anyway.

I closed the box, then lifted it, carrying it from the stock room and out to the front counter. I plunked it down, then put my elegant and handy *"back in fifteen minutes"* sign on the door.

I needed to see if there were more unsent letters in that box. Or replies. I needed to see what else was in there, too. And in the second box, besides. I was probably going to need to take the boxes home to get through them all.

But first?

I picked up the cold mug of coffee and headed to the back again, but to the kitchenette this time.

To get through this, I was going to need more caffeine, stat. And maybe a cookie or two.

CHAPTER 12
Marsha

WE WERE at my favorite store in the neighborhood. Bones, Dogs, and Harmony was bright, cheerful, and smelled like heaven. Liver treats. Dried fish snacks for the cats. Rawhide bones.

And toys! Oh, the toys! Rubber balls. Plushies that squeaked. Frisbees. All sorts of wonderful things that filled my corgi heart with joy.

There were also records, which I didn't understand. I mean, music is okay, but it doesn't hold a candle to treats.

There were only two things in the shop that Klaus and I hated: the African Gray parrot who lived in a giant enclosure in the front window, and the collection of dog and cat clothing. Ugh. I especially hated the raincoats Garrett bought for us last winter. Klaus and I dragged them into the back garden, chewed and tore them, then trampled them in the mud.

We were filthy, but wow did that feel satisfying. Garrett never made us wear raincoats after that.

Fancy collars and the occasional bowtie were acceptable. Sweaters and coats? No.

"Hey fellas! Hey Marsha. Hey Klaus!"

Ron was the best human ever. He was warm, and large, with a big belly always covered in soft T-shirts or sweaters, and had long dark hair twisted into what John called "locks." His skin was a warm brown, and so were his big eyes behind their round gold-rimmed glasses.

And he smelled like cinnamon and dog treats.

I sighed in contentment, licked his outstretched hand in greeting. I also said hello to Fred, an ancient black lab half snoozing on a dog bed behind the counter. He raised his head in greeting, then went back to sleep.

Then, tail wagging, I trotted off toward the toy section. I knew John and Garrett would buy our favorite treats, so I didn't need to worry about that. But unless I already had my jaws wrapped around a toy, they might not buy us one of those.

"Come on, Klaus!"

"In a minute!" Klaus barked. I looked over my shoulder. Klaus was busy getting his little tan head scratched by Ron, his own tail wagging in bliss. I didn't blame Klaus. Ron was a class A head scratcher.

Klaus joined me, and soon enough we were nose deep in an assortment of toys. There were bins of balls. Plushies hung from racks low to the ground at corgi height.

Did I mention how much I love and admire Ron?

Klaus sniffed each toy delicately. He's pickier than I am about his toys. I don't know why. We're just going to chew them to death. Maybe I should ask.

"Why are you so picky about your toys?" I asked.

He paused in his examination of a red octopus plushie.

"Some smell better than others. Some of them have a nice texture. Some of them seem like they'd be good to chew. And other ones?" He shrugged his little shoulders. *"I just like them."*

Fair enough.

I grabbed a pink ball with chewy spines from the ball box and left Klaus to his perusal.

Trotting happily back to the front of the store, I wove around a few customers, including one woman with a tabby cat in a harness. The woman was flipping through Ron's record collection. Records are old-fashioned forms of music, which is why Garrett likes them. He likes anything old fashioned. John had talked Garrett out of starting a record collection, calling them "pretentious."

The cat glared at me from its perch on the woman's shoulder, green eyes narrowing. But it didn't say anything, so I ignored it.

I'd found with cats that it was best to not provoke them. And I'd also learned the hard way that almost any old thing could provoke a cat.

"We think Saschi was blackmailing people," Garrett was saying. He kept his voice soft, like he didn't want anyone else in the store to hear.

"Oh, man." Ron shook his head, then took off his wire-rimmed glasses to rub at his eyes, like he was tired. "I hate to hear that, but I've gotta tell you, I'm not surprised."

"Surprise!" The African gray yelled from the window.

"Settle down there, Josephine Baker," Ron said, but his voice was mild. I'd never heard him raise his voice to anyone, even when he must be really mad.

"Why aren't you surprised?" John asked. I wanted to know, too.

"Saschi was always into everyone else's tea. Like, more than most. And sometimes they'd have this look in their eye like they were storing stuff away, you know?"

Storing stuff away. I knew all about that. Even though John and Garrett were good about keeping the house clean and tidy, Klaus and I had a space between one of the chairs closest to the fireplace and the wall. We kept a lot of toys there.

If we didn't, John would never let us buy more every time we came to Ron's store.

But the toys weren't exactly secrets. We just hoped John and Garrett would forget about them.

Though maybe that's what secrets were to humans, hidden toys. I didn't think so, though. The kind of secrets they were talking about seemed more serious.

More dangerous somehow.

Like some people had done some very bad things. Or things that John sometimes said we should be ashamed of.

Though that baby wasn't using her teddy bear, was she? And it was right there in her stroller, at mouth height.

I peeked around the counter. Fred cracked one eye open.

"Fred, do you know any secrets humans have been keeping?"

The old lab sighed. *"Humans always have secrets. You just have to know where to look."*

By the time I formed an answer, he was snoring again, so I settled in to chew on the new ball and listen to the humans.

"So, you really think Saschi was killed by someone they were blackmailing?" Ron was saying.

"I'm not sure. But we should let you get back to your

other customers," Garrett said. I noticed he didn't mention the letter, though. That was curious.

"Klaus!" Garrett called toward the back.

Klaus was really taking a long time. Ridiculous.

"But if you hear anything else, you'll shoot us a text?" John asked.

"Well, shoot *me* a text," Garrett interjected. "John never checks his phone."

Ron rumbled with a laugh. "I found that out when I was organizing the neighborhood barbecue last summer. You got your head in your own world, man. But keep at it. When's the next book out?"

John brightened. "Next month, actually. And I'm already halfway through the next one in the series."

"I'm glad you're a fast writer. Keep me in my main addiction besides my animals, here."

Klaus trotted up with the red octopus.

Ron peered over the counter. "You two pick out what you want? Hmm. A pink ball and a red octopus. Good choices."

John grabbed the toys from us so Ron could ring them up.

"And a bag of liver treats, please," Garrett said.

"You took all that time to choose that octopus? Why? Wasn't it the first toy you saw?"

Klaus sneezed. I backed away from the spray.

My little tan and white friend licked his black nose and said, *"I don't know what I want until I see everything. Just because you'll take any old toy, doesn't mean I can't be more discriminating."*

I would have replied, but John handed me back my ball, so my mouth was full.

But I still didn't know why Klaus had to examine every last toy when he was just going to pick the one right in front of his face.

Wait a minute… maybe we were missing something. Something important. And it was right in front of our faces.

I just wished I knew what it was.

CHAPTER 13
Garrett

THE SUN WAS GONE, and April rain pattered softly from a gray Portland sky. My garden would be so happy. The pups were at home today, keeping John company as he figured out a way to stop a ticking bomb, or whatever peril he was putting his characters through.

I swear, that man of mine has a twisty, twisty brain inside his beautiful head.

Me? I'm a lot simpler. I love a clean line, the sweep of velvet and the curve of wood. As long as it is pre-1980, I'll get all heart eyes about it.

The street outside the shop was quiet and I hummed along to some Tori Amos as I worked. I paused to get up and stretch my legs. Carrying my teacup with me, I wandered the store, making sure everything was in place. Klaus and Marsha were pretty good in the shop, but that didn't mean one of them hadn't decided to drag a cushion behind a sofa somewhere.

I'd dusted the day before, so things looked good on that front. I wandered toward the mid-century modern section of the store. Yarrow had decided against the orange crackle glaze lamps set on the sleek wood night stands, but said they might be back for a chair. After the Craftsman era, mid-mod was my favorite.

A splash of green caught my eye from beneath one of the low-slung chairs. I'd just reupholstered them in a rich goldenrod weave, so the green stood out in contrast. Crouching down, I peered beneath the chair. The green was writing on a black button, the kind a person would pin to a jacket or the strap of a backpack.

"Still Here, Still Queer," it read. It reminded me of the old buttons from the 1990s. Queer Nation and all that. I was a kid back then but had a fondness for the era. My parents had made sure I was imprinted on 90s music.

The queer stuff? Not so much. But that's why I live in the city, isn't it? Rural Oregon doesn't spell LGBTQ too well, let alone the other, newer additions to the alphabet.

I wondered who had dropped the thing. Could have been anyone. Yarrow was the only person who specifically asked about the mid-mod section, but browsers tended to wander the whole store, seeing what tchotchkes called to them.

I'd need to ask Yarrow next time I saw them.

The electronic chime above the front door sounded, letting in the scent of fresh, spring rain.

"Hello? Garrett?"

"Coming!"

I recognized that voice. It sounded strained. When I rounded a 1920s era armoire, I saw that the face was strained, too.

"Princess Sparkle Toes, are you okay?"

Princess Sparkle Toes was a formidable presence.

White, Jewish, and six feet tall in her sensible low heeled, knee-high black boots, today she wore a hot pink trench coat and as usual, had a full face of makeup, with contoured cheekbones and a smoky eye. At eleven in the morning.

Mascara ran down her pale, perfectly made-up face, but I didn't think it was from the rain.

"I'm not feeling so sparkly today," she said, plum painted lips turned down.

My nose twitched a little. She wore a rose water scent, which I usually found pleasing, but she'd applied it with a heavy hand.

PST, as we sometimes called her, was yet another gender fluid queer in our overcrowded little village-in-the-city. Some days PST's pronouns were he, some days, she. At least with her, we could tell by the clothing and amount of make-up. But the name stayed ever the same. She was Sparkle Toes in boy or girl mode, and loved loved *loved* to get her heart broken by handsome men.

Or so she said.

And it certainly looked as if someone had broken her heart today.

"PST! What happened? Are you okay?"

I rushed toward her, arms open, and she fell across my shoulders, sobbing into my green tweed blazer.

The trouble with being 5'7" is that I'm often surrounded by people wearing heels, which means I'm often being draped over. And when John is in drag? I feel like a kindly Hobbit or something, with an elven princess on my arm. John in heels is both gorgeous and ridiculous.

Not that I'm complaining. Much.

I let PST cry for a while, before patting her back.

"Why don't I put the kettle on, and we can have a chat about what's bothering you?"

I limited myself to one cup of coffee a day, but so far could get away with drinking all the tea I wanted up until two o'clock. John badgered me to drink more actual water, and he was right. So, I'd started compromising with switching out my cups of English Breakfast with mint or rooibos or some other herbal blends.

"It's that bitch, Yarrow!" PST wailed, stomping toward my favorite 1940s velvet chairs.

Uh oh. No time for tea, then. I followed her and sat down.

"What happened?"

PST looked at me as if I had two heads.

"They killed Saschi! And now they're going around town acting all sad."

PST's mouth was set in a mulish line, eyes boring into me as if I shared her anger.

"I don't understand," I said, keeping my voice gentle, as if Sparkle Toes was a skittish horse. "I thought Yarrow and Saschi were friends."

She snorted, sounding a little bit like Bruiser. "As if. Yarrow would pretend that. But it isn't true."

PST looked out the windows at the falling rain, then picked up an old leather-bound book from the coffee table, running her fingers across the surface as if she could read it for clues. I noticed the hot pink polish on her left pointer finger was chipped.

She really must have been upset. One thing you could count on with Sparkle Toes? Her manicure was always on fleek. Or whatever the current slang was. Once I hit forty, I stopped keeping up.

I sat quietly and just waited. John told me recently that if you kept quiet, people would tell you a lot more about themselves than you sometimes wanted to know.

"At least, not lately," she continued. "They'd been fighting like cats and dogs. Yarrow said Saschi had betrayed them."

I sat up straight. "What do you mean, betrayed them?"

PST dug in the black leather bag at her side, whipping out a compact and a tissue. Tilting her head toward the window, she began to dab at her face, trying to wipe away the mascara streaks without causing further damage to her perfect contour makeup.

I swear, I appreciate the beauty of femmes, but am glad I'm a soft butch dandy. My shoe bill is lower—even though I've got expensive taste—and I don't have to wear makeup. Once I'm dressed for the day, with a little pomade in my seal brown hair, I'm good to go for hours unless I spill coffee on myself, or Klaus and Marsha get into something particularly messy and disgusting.

Once again, I waited for Sparkle Toes to finish her thought. I tapped a finger on my black trousers, wishing I'd put the kettle on after all. I discreetly checked the vintage gold watch at my wrist. Just because it was a slow day in the store, didn't mean there wasn't a pile of work to be done. Both of my current clients needed to be kept apprised of their projects, and I still had fabrics to choose for the soft furnishings for client number one.

"Sparkle Toes?" I asked, breaking into her repair job. She looked at me, brown eyes startled as if she'd forgotten I was there. "What do you mean Saschi betrayed Yarrow?"

She shrugged, then unbuttoned her pink trench coat, revealing a tasteful burgundy knit dress. A gold Star of

David rested in the vee of the neckline and matched the gold hoops in her ears.

"Sparkle Toes, I can't help you if you don't tell me what's on your mind." And I might not be able to help even then. And did I want to help?

I mean, I had work to do, and a life to lead. Why was I enmeshed in this mess in the first place?

Because you saw Saschi lying on the restaurant floor, and now they're dead.

Right. Good reason.

CHAPTER 14
Marsha

JOHN WAS IN THE KITCHEN, making a sandwich for lunch. Klaus and I were underfoot, vying for a piece of ham. John turned from the big, shiny black refrigerator that Garrett said was "retro style" though it seemed new to me. A head of lettuce in one hand and a jar of mustard in the other, he almost tripped over Klaus.

"Klaus! Marsha!"

Why was I in trouble? I was sitting innocently, tail wagging, a full two nose lengths away. Klaus was the one who'd nosed right up to the fridge.

"How many times do I have to tell you, you can't get so close when I'm moving around the kitchen. What if I'd had something hot in my hands?"

He couldn't fool me. Humans did not keep hot things in the refrigerator. Hot things came from the oven and the stove, and both Klaus and I knew to not get close when those were on.

We only needed that lesson once.

From the counter, John's phone buzzed. He glanced at it, then started washing lettuce.

"That's Jacki from Bruiser's," he said, talking to us while constructing his sandwich. The smell of ham and cheddar was driving me bonkers.

"*Cheese!*" Klaus barked.

"*Cheese! Cheese!*" I barked. "*Ham and cheese!*"

"Okay. Okay. Calm down. I know what you're asking for." John cut two pieces of cheese from the block and handed one to me and one to Klaus.

I gobbled it in one bite. Stingy. Didn't he know by now that I could eat a lot more cheese than that? I mean, I know to humans. Klaus and I look small, but we're very sturdy and could pack away a lot of treats if only they gave us the chance.

"Jacki wants to know if we can come by. What do you think? Want a walk in the rain after lunch? Go visit Bruiser?"

I wagged my tail and looked as happy as I could. Walks in the rain weren't always my favorite, but seeing Bruiser was worth it.

"*Yes!*" Klaus barked. Klaus liked walks in the rain. He didn't mind his coat getting damp and even loved splashing through puddles, despite the fact that it got the white parts of his fur dirty.

Call me a prima donna, but I preferred to stay dry. But since my humans live in rainy Oregon, I didn't have much choice. Walks in the rain it was.

John made short work of his lunch while Klaus and I alternately gazed up at him adoringly and lapped at our water dishes, making sure to rattle the empty food bowls while we were at it. He ignored us, a paper book propped open on the table, eating that delicious sandwich without offering us even one bite.

Finally, the kitchen was clean, his plate in the dishwasher, and he was putting on his rain jacket and grabbing our leashes.

"You sure you guys don't want your raincoats?"

As soon as he said it, I began to back away. He laughed, eyes crinkling at the corners.

"All right. Message received. If you want to get wet, that's up to you." He shoved a small towel into his backpack though. That was nice. It meant we could dry off at Bruiser's and not have to sit around wet and miserable.

And there were always dog cookies at Bruiser's, so that made it worthwhile.

Soon enough, we were walking down the sidewalk. The rain smelled good, even though it washed away some of the other more interesting smells. Which made me wonder…

"Hey, Klaus!"

"Yeah?" Klaus trotted beside me, head swiveling right to left, looking for interesting trash. Our neighborhood didn't have much except down some of the alleyways, but Klaus was always hopeful there would be some decaying thing to paw through. Sometimes he even rolls in that stuff. He's kind of disgusting that way.

"Outside the restaurant, did you *smell anything unusual?"* I'd been wracking my little brain about that, and it still bothered me. I felt like I should have smelled something off, but all I smelled were Saschi's weird smell, the ordinary food smells, and then the bushes outside.

I mean, the place was filled with people, and they all

had a scent, but had anyone smelled weird somehow? Besides Saschi?

"Just bushes. That plastic vial didn't smell like much. Maybe a little bit like old fish, but mostly just plastic."

The vial smelled like old fish? Well. That was interesting. Maybe Saschi had dropped it. But Yarrow had said it couldn't be theirs.

We were really moving now, walking as fast as we could to get out of the rain. Klaus had even stopped his exploring and was nosing ahead, aiming for the corner we turned at to get to Bruiser's.

"Except," he said, *"something smelled like a rose bush."*

I stopped, almost tripping John.

"Hey! What in the world, Marsha P?"

"Sorry!" I woofed and got moving again.

I turned to Klaus, who glanced over at me.

"There aren't any rose bushes at the sushi restaurant."

His eyes grew big, but he didn't say anything, just increased his speed.

That must be another clue! I was excited. First the vial, then the smell of roses! Just wait until I told Bruiser!

At the café, John shucked off the hood of his jacket and slung his backpack off. Crouching just inside the door on the big black carpet that came out on rainy days, he carefully wiped our paws, then rubbed us down. It felt good to be dry again.

"You two, stay at the table here with Bruiser. And be good!"

He loped off to the counter. I hoped he remembered to get us cookies.

I touched noses with Bruiser, who wheezed at me. He

wagged his little stump, causing his whole rear end to wiggle.

"*Hey!*" he said. "*You came to visit!*"

"*Hey yourself,*" Klaus replied. "*Jacki needed to see John.*"

Bruiser nodded. "*Oh, yeah. Jacki and Bex have both been in a bother all morning. I don't know what's wrong. Something about that person you found?*"

He turned his big wet eyes my way. A string of slobber hung from the left side of his mouth. Gross. I tried to not look at it, but it was mesmerizing, the way it almost broke and dropped to the floor, but then didn't.

Ugh.

"*What are they saying?*" Klaus asked, unbothered by Bruiser's drool.

Bruiser plopped his barrel body down onto the floor beneath the table. "*A man came in this morning and talked to Bex. Was accusing Saschi about all sorts of things.*"

Bruiser's voice trailed off, as if he'd lost the string. His eyes closed. Was he actually taking a nap in the middle of our conversation?

"*Then what?*" I asked.

He snorted, jerking awake, those red-rimmed eyes startled.

"*Then what?*" he asked, repeating my words.

I wanted to bite his white legs. Klaus put a paw over mine, as if warning me to calm down. Had I growled?

Bruiser looked a little scared. Okay. Maybe I had growled.

"*You were saying a man was accusing Saschi of things.*" And then you fell asleep. "*Then what happened?*"

"*Oh! He got a panini and a coffee to go. Stormed out of the place. Didn't even scratch my head.*"

"What did he smell like?"

Good question, Klaus! Maybe he was catching on.

"Hard to tell over the panini and coffee. But now that you mention it, he smelled a little funny. Like cigarettes."

We all twitched our noses. Not many people smoked cigarettes, and we hated it when people walked by, polluting the air.

"Didn't Garrett say it was a vial of nicotine? And isn't that what cigarettes have?" I asked.

Klaus sat up, ears alert, then slumped again, dejected. *"But the vial didn't smell like cigarettes."*

Roses. A plastic vial. Angry, upset people. A letter. And one dead waiter.

I lay down and rested my nose on my paws.

Nothing added up. But at least I'd had a piece of cheese, and a cookie was on its way.

Soon, I hoped.

CHAPTER 15

Garrett

I COULDN'T STOP CHECKING my watch. Any minute now, and Princess Sparkle Toes would notice and take offense.

"Sparkle Toes, you have to tell me. Was Yarrow threatening anyone? Or did they just have a fight with Saschi?"

I mean, people fought all the time, over the silliest things. It was one reason John and I were so stable. We didn't let the petty stuff fester and blow up. We'd get annoyed with each other, sure. But then we'd work it out. Our only real fights were about important things. Those fights were hard for me at first. I was so scared he would reject me. Leave me. At times, I was tempted to leave myself, just to be the first one to walk away.

But then one day he explained that honest conflict was a way to get closer to each other if we let it. That sometimes we trounced on each other's baggage, but that didn't mean the relationship was over. It just meant we got to figure out more about the other person along the way.

And then I went to therapy for a couple of years to get help managing my rejection sensitivity.

I still didn't like those kinds of fights, and luckily they were rare, but I no longer felt completely terrified that someone I loved would kick me out of our home just for being me.

"It wasn't just a fight." PST had shredded one tissue and was working hard on shredding a second. There was a mounting pile on the coffee table that I hoped to clean up before any paying customers entered the store.

The chimes sounded again, and Roderick Gauge stormed in, face as cloudy as the great Oregon outdoors. His black rain jacket swirled around him, and his face and glasses were wet. He stopped just inside the door to wipe the lenses, shoved the glasses back on his pasty white face, and jerked his head around the store.

His eyes fell on me, then on Sparkle Toes, who straightened her spine and set her mouth in a line.

I braced for impact, hoping the explosion wouldn't be too huge. Like I said, not a big fan of conflict.

"You!" he said, pointing a finger at Sparkle Toes and stalking toward us, dripping all the way.

I sighed. Why didn't he shake off his jacket and wipe his feet? I was going to need to mop the aisle now.

"What about me?" PST said, hoisting her sharp chin into the air like a cruise ship flag.

"You killed Saschi! Don't deny it! You were there that day! I saw you!"

Whoa. Wait a minute. Had I seen Sparkle Toes or Roderick while we were eating dinner? I scrolled through my memories, frantically searching.

Roderick was upon us now, still wagging that finger.

He crouched as though about to sit on the velvet covered sofa.

"Stop!" I shouted, leaping up from my chair.

They both paused, startled, and looked at me.

"Don't sit on the velvet with wet clothing, please!"

"She's sitting in her trench coat!" Roderick pointed out.

"Trench coats don't shed water the same way as your jacket." Did I really need to point this out to two queers? What was wrong with people? I'm not exactly fashion forward, but I still know my fabrics. Sheesh.

"Fine!" Roderick snapped, shucking his jacket as he walked back to the door. He flung it on the coat rack by the counter, which, I might point out, was there for that very purpose, and wiped his feet like an angry bull on the industrial carpet I left in the front during rainy season.

Too little, too late, but better than nothing, I guess.

Sparkle Toes rose and was buttoning her coat. She picked up her big leather bag and flung it over one shoulder.

"No, you don't!" Roderick was fuming. "You are not walking out of this conversation!"

"I don't have to stay and be yelled at!" she yelled back.

I held my head in my hands.

"Do you really need to fight in my store?"

They both whirled on me as if I was the one to blame. I sighed and plunked my butt back on the chair.

"Sit down. Both of you. Let's talk this out like two adults."

"Why should I speak with this person who just accused me of murder?"

Ugh. Forget coffee or tea. What I needed was a large

piece of chocolate cake. Or a vacation. Preferably some-place with a lot of museums.

"Please," I said. "Just sit. Both of you. Let's talk this out."

Roderick parked his black jeans on the sofa as Sparkle Toes gingerly sat on the edge of her chair. I gave her a look. She rolled her eyes and scooted back so she no longer looked as if she was about to dash for the door. She even took that ridiculously large bag off her shoulder.

I leaned forward, elbows on my knees, and looked from one to the other. Both of them were trying their darn-dest to look both affronted and superior. But behind that? I could sense a deep well of pain.

And maybe guilt. What was that about?

"Look," I said. "I know you're both upset, but let's not take it out on each other, okay? Saschi was special. I get it. I liked Saschi, too."

"I *loved* Saschi," PST sniffed. "They were like a sibling to me."

Roderick set his jaw and looked past her shoulder, out at the still-falling rain.

"A lot of us loved Saschi," he said. "But a lot of us hated them, too."

Now we were getting somewhere. Or not. First, PST had accused Yarrow, and then Roderick accused Princess Sparkle Toes? Well, maybe I wasn't sure exactly where we were getting.

I sat back, rubbing my fingers along the velvet arm of the chair. I needed all the soothing I could get to deal with these two.

Okay. I mentally girded my loins. May as well strike at the heart of the matter and see what happened.

"Who was Saschi blackmailing?"

Sparkle Toes gasped, a thin hand flying to her flat chest. And Roderick burst into tears.

"Me," he croaked out. "Saschi was blackmailing me!"

"What?" Both Sparkle Toes and I blurted.

Roderick held his face in his hands for a moment. Sparkle Toes looked at me and raised one perfect eyebrow, but said nothing.

I grabbed a tissue from the box and held it toward him.

"Here."

He looked up, nodded, and plucked the tissue from my hand, blowing his nose noisily. I handed him a second tissue, which he used to mop his face.

Didn't anyone carry handkerchiefs anymore? Besides me, I mean. But I didn't have enough for all these people and their waterworks.

"Tell us what happened," I said.

He nodded again, crumpling the tissues in his hand.

"We were lovers, a long time ago. Back when I had a tiny drug habit."

He held up a hand to forestall questions.

"I did cocaine for two years. I haven't touched it, or anything else, including alcohol, since."

"And Saschi was holding this over you?" That surprised me. I mean, addiction happens. And in a community of people like ours? Sometimes it happens a lot. White collar workers are some of the most affected, by the way. And all those people on the streets? If they're on drugs, for most of them, the drug use came after they became homeless.

"No. Not the coke." He looked from me to Princess

Sparkle Toes. "This can't leave this room. No one else knows, so if it spreads? I'll know who to blame."

"Agreed," I said. "Sparkle Toes?"

She held out for a second, but quickly nodded. "Agreed."

Roderick tapped a finger on his jeans, staring out the window once again, as if he didn't want to look at us while he told his tale.

"I started stealing from work. Embezzling. Just a little bit. Small amounts from a variety of accounts."

"You were a what? Bank manager or something?" I asked.

"I'm a CPA. Or I used to be. I did payroll for a local firm. I've been relegated to freelance accounting work these days," he said, mouth set in a grimace.

That sounded rough.

"What happened?" PST asked.

"I got caught. And they should have fired me. But the CEO had a daughter who died from drugs. He gave me a chance. I could enter rehab, then take a demotion, but I'd have a job to return to. And he would garnish my wages privately, until all the money was paid back. I did it, but then couldn't face working there anymore. The shame was too great."

Wow. What a story. But something still was not adding up.

"If your boss already knew," I asked, "what was Saschi holding over you?"

Sparkle Toes cleared her throat. "I think I know."

She turned her gaze on Roderick. "She was threatening to tell the library, wasn't she?"

Roderick raised his chin and squared his shoulders.

"Wait. Library? I don't get it." I had been following the thread but was now completely confused.

PST explained. "Roderick is part of Storytime for Us All. People of all types and walks of life take a day to read aloud to kids. The program has become so popular, it's expanding. And Roderick was part of that. Weren't you?"

"I *am* part of that," he corrected, voice fierce. "I read to kids every Wednesday afternoon and was on the expansion committee. Anyway, Saschi was threatening to tell the library board."

"And?" I asked.

"I went in and told them myself. They said as long as I was paying back the debt—you know, making things right—I was welcome back as a reader. The kids like me, and so does the library board."

His voice was quiet, but firm. Okay. So, in fifteen minutes he'd been added to my suspect list, and maybe, possibly, removed from it again.

I checked my watch. My client was coming in five minutes.

Crap.

"I hate to cut this short, you two, but I've got a client coming any minute. I need you both gone."

This was client number two. I hoped they'd be able to shed light on the color choices they wanted, because I was still struggling to figure it out from the information they'd sent me.

They rose swiftly and thanked me for my time. Roderick grabbed his coat, and Sparkle Toes buttoned her pink trench. The bell chimed as the door closed behind them.

It was only after they had both left that I realized something important.

I never found out why Roderick had accused Princess Sparkle Toes of murder. No. She had shifted the conversation onto him before I could find out.

And then I remembered something else. There'd been a person in a pink coat at the hospital the night Saschi collapsed.

A pink coat that looked an awful lot like the trench coat Princess Sparkle Toes wore.

CHAPTER 16

Adam

EVERYONE HAD COME HOME in a tizzy. The dogs scrabbled around, barking, as John and Garrett held an equally excited conversation.

I eased my way downstairs, temporarily forgetting that my big leather boots no longer made noise on the old wooden stairs. Those stairs used to groan in protest throughout the day and night, what with all our comings and goings. Work. Rallies. Protests. Parties. Bringing lovers home. Shooing those same lovers back out the door in the morning.

I smiled at the memories.

John and Garrett didn't make as much noise as we had. For one thing, there were only two of them. For another, they didn't wear shoes inside the house. Probably smart, though I can't say it's a thing I ever thought about before.

And now the boots I was so proud of, and kept polished to a high shine, left no tracks. Being dead is very strange.

"The nicotine!" Marsha was barking when I strolled from the dining room into the kitchen.

"And roses!" Klaus chimed in.

"Hush, you two!" John scolded. "I'll get your dinner in a minute. Just let me finish putting these groceries away."

Garrett was rinsing tomatoes at the sink, getting ready to prep dinner, as John unloaded two canvas bags into the cupboards and big black, retro looking fridge.

They'd done a great job with the place, I had to admit. Garrett was quite the designer. The small man had managed to retain all the character and features that made the old house its own, while updating things just enough that it all worked better. That was quite a feat, and I bet his business was very successful because of it.

"What did Bex say?" Garrett asked, setting the colander filled with small red orbs aside. He plucked some green leaves from a plant on the kitchen windowsill. I couldn't smell anymore, but from memory, it looked like basil.

The sky was still light outside the big window over the sink, but the rain clouds were bringing night's gloom pretty quickly. Rain. I missed the feel of it on my skin. I missed the feel of sun, too. And another man's lips pressed to mine.

Sweet moments. I missed those. Like the way John gently brushed Garrett's shoulder as he passed behind him. The way the dogs pranced in excitement as John spooned disgusting looking wet food in their bowls, giving them each a pat on the head as they noisily chowed down.

Life. I missed life. I can see, but it's all got a tinge of gray to it. And I can hear, though sound is slightly muffled. Taste and scent are more memory than anything, and faded memory at that.

But I have to say, after all the things we fought for? It fills my heart with joy to see two men together, doing the simple chores that keep life going. Two men and their dogs.

"Bex said that Enrico came in, yelling. He said Saschi had stolen something from him and for some reason he thought they would have it." John answered.

He leaned against the counter now, drinking water from a tumbler as Garrett salted water for the box of pasta sitting on the white quartz.

"Enrico, Enrico? Like, from Enrico's?" Garrett asked.

"One and the same."

I had no idea what Enrico's was. It hadn't existed while I was alive.

"Did he say what Saschi stole?"

John shook his head. "No. But he insisted that Bex knew all about it, and that she and Jacki were in cahoots with Saschi and wanted to ruin his club."

Ah. A nightclub. I wondered what kind.

"In cahoots?" Garrett laughed. "Did he actually say that?"

John smiled. "Apparently, he did. I mean, I like Enrico, but he's a bit eccentric."

Garrett dumped dried noodles into the boiling water.

"As if everyone in this place isn't eccentric. Including us."

"Hey! Speak for yourself!"

John stepped across the kitchen and gave Garrett a squeeze. "You're the eccentric one of the family, with your tweed jackets and bow ties, my handsome man."

Garrett turned in his arms, looking up at John's face. "And what are you then?"

"I am but a humble writer of thrillers and mysteries. I simple person, trying to earn my bread."

John plucked a cherry tomato from the colander and popped it in his mouth.

Garrett swatted John away as he reached for a second, round red orb. "Those are for the pasta. And as soon as I heat the oil, they're going in the pan."

He slid a large skillet on the gas burner next to the noodle pot and turned the heat on low before reaching for a large bottle of olive oil.

I groaned. The memory of pasta with nothing but salt, oil, fresh tomato and basil suddenly hitting me. My lover Luis used to make the exact same dish. "Peasant pasta," he called it.

It was the best thing in the world.

"At any rate," John said, moving out of Garrett's way, he went to lean against the sink, "Bex and Jacki have no clue what he's talking about, but said he was very angry. After Bex got him to leave, he paced outside, vaping out clouds, and glaring into the café. When Jacki asked him to take his noxious cloud elsewhere, he about punched her in the face. Bex had to rush out to intervene."

"And Bruiser almost bit him!" Marsha barked.

I wondered what in the world vaping was. Sounded like a form of smoking. Things had changed since I'd been gone. Used to be, clove cigarettes were all in vogue. That spicy sweet smell was another memory that took me back.

"Bruiser said Bex and Jacki were very upset!" Klaus barked.

"What now, you two?" John asked. "We just got back

from a walk, and I'm not taking you out again in this rain. You need to go out, the dog door is right there." He pointed toward the back of the kitchen, through a door frame, into what we used to use as an extra pantry. It was now kitted up as a small mud room, with a bench and hooks. Sure enough, the garden door had a doggie flap cut into it.

"Vaping?" Garrett asked. "Are you thinking what I'm thinking? Coming through. Boiling water."

Garrett hoisted the pot using two red mitts and, bracing his arms, staggered toward the big sink as John scrambled out of his way, plopping the now empty colander into the sink at the last minute.

A cloud of steam rose in the air.

"Yeah," John said, over the sound of running water as Garrett rinsed the noodles. He walked over to the stove to give the tomatoes and basil a quick stir. "Vaping."

Garrett turned, face flushed with the heat. "Well, it's Friday night. I wanted to stay in because of the rain, but…"

"Enrico's it is. I have just the frock for it."

A pang of longing hit my heart. A Friday night out at a club. It had been so long…

But I'm stuck here in this house. Guess I'll be babysitting the dogs.

CHAPTER 17
Garrett

THE CLUB WAS ALREADY JAM PACKED and noisy, even though it was only going on nine. Self-proclaimed Mayor Sweetheart Digs was holding court at a booth in the back corner, trying to compete with up-and-coming drag queen Mary Contrary in flash and flamboyance. I didn't want to know who was going to win that contest but would keep an eye on them all the same. As far as I was concerned, Sweetheart Digs was still on my list of suspects.

John looked gorgeous in an orange frock that skimmed his thin frame, flaring out at his hips and ending just above his knees. He wore a towering brown wig, early-1960s style, and black eyeliner flicked up at the corner of his brown eyes, making cat eyes. He wore contact lenses tonight, and his eyes were huge. His lips were painted a complementary orange. He wouldn't let me kiss him until the night was through.

"Anticipation is the best sauce," he said when he caught me staring. "And it's a good thing I can pull myself together in an hour. I can't believe you made us come out this early."

I scanned the crowd, searching for a place to park ourselves.

"You know I have to work tomorrow morning. Unlike writers, who can wake up whenever they please, some of us have real jobs."

He poked me in the ribs, and I laughed. John made more money than I did, barely, but still. And he worked hard every day, both writing and running his small publishing business.

"Besides," I said, "this place is already packed. Any later, and we would never get seats."

It was definitely Queers Night Out at Enrico's. A sparkly curtain hung across the small stage at the rear of the club. Coat check and washrooms to the left, offices to the right.

Queens towered in their heels, and dapper butches preened. A raucous group of cis women hogged three corner tables. Must be a bachelorette party, the bane of drag bar existence, along with bringing in a lot of bread and butter.

I gestured John closer. "There's a table over there! Want me to score it, and you get the drinks? Or vice versa?"

He pursed his tangerine painted lips, eyes narrowing.

"Kitty and Rafael are at the table next to that one. I'll go. Get me whatever cocktail looks the most dangerous, okay?"

I grinned and gave my lover a thumbs up. He kissed my cheek and sashayed on his way, greeting friends in the crowd.

Like I said, for a person who stays at home all day, he

sure is popular and happy about it. Whereas I, a neurodivergent introvert, have to deal with the general public for a living. Go figure.

The cosmos is good for a laugh.

I threaded my own way through the crowd. My eye fell on Roderick and Princess Sparkle Toes having a heated conversation near the hallway by the stage. Guess he was still mad. But something about that whole situation bothered me.

"Garrett!" Bex practically bounced in her Doc Martens. She'd paired the boots with a short black skirt, and an off the shoulder soft white shirt showed off a tattooed swallow in the dip of each shoulder. Bex used to travel a lot before she and Jacki opened the café. The swallows were some sort of equator crossing talisman that came from sailors.

"Where's Jacki?" I bellowed. The music was loud. Just in the time that I'd been here, it had shifted from Lizzo to Taylor Swift, and now on to some techno-beat dance club stuff that I had no clue about, but from the whoops that came up from the crowd on the dance floor, it was something popular.

Bex leaned in. "She's getting our drinks. I was just heading back to help her."

I nodded and motioned her forward, following her white shirt through the crowd of happy people.

A glass smashed behind me, and I swore I heard a snarl. Huh. Maybe not so happy. My head whipped around, and I saw Sparkle Toes clomping off in platform shoes.

Roderick was nowhere to be seen, but Daniel from

How We Roll leaned against the wall, a smirk on his face. When had he arrived?

Everyone seemed to be here except for Enrico, the man we'd come to see. The man who should be on the floor, making sure his club was running smoothly.

I turned again, almost smashing into Bex's back. She'd stopped, one yard from the long wood sweep of the bar.

"Bex?" I asked the question in her ear.

When she turned her head to look at me, her eyes were wide.

"Bex? What's wrong?"

She shook her head. "Nothing. It's nothing. Just thought I saw someone I used to know. Come on. Jacki's right over there."

We excused and smiled our way through the crush, but my smile, at least, was fake. Bex was lying to me. But why? And whom had she seen?

Jacki was just about to hoist a full pint glass and some ruby colored cocktail when she caught sight of us. She looked good tonight in a raspberry blazer and a patterned head wrap in burgundy and blue. She smiled at Bex, then frowned. Bex's face must still be giving something away.

Something I needed to find out.

"Hey, Garrett!" Jacki grinned at me. A short woman in a sparkling mini dress stood next to Jacki with her back to me, her hair a blonde cloud around her head. Jacki was making a weird motion with her head, trying to signal something to Bex.

"What's going on?" I said to Jacki, trying to shove myself closer to the crowded sweep of wood. The bartenders, one a burly white man whose black T-shirt strained across his gym-built chest, and the other, a tall

Black woman who wore a striped vest loose over a white singlet. Jerome and Ace. I knew them both well. Ace looked up at me and quirked a pierced eyebrow. She wore jewelry everywhere. Eyebrow piercing. Nose ring. Mounds of beaded necklaces and a stack of bracelets up her arms. I had no clue how she even moved under all the weight, but move she did, fast as lightning, bottles spinning like gyroscopes.

But before I could place my order, reflected in the long mirror behind the shelves of liquor, all shining like jewels in the nightclub lights, I saw the blonde woman's face.

Vyviane. The woman who ripped my heart from my chest and stomped it to the ground. No wonder Bex and Jacki were acting so weird.

Sweat dotted my upper lip, and my heart pounded.

Breathe, Garrett. She can't hurt you anymore.

But I thought she'd left town for good, off to fish in a bigger lake. Our queer village is small, and I didn't relish running into her everywhere. I exhaled out a big sigh, leaned past two men kissing, and shouted my order at Ace.

"A Ransom Gin martini, extra olives, and whatever cocktail you think will strike John's fancy."

Ace winked at me. "Coming up."

Time to face the music. And not the Lil Nas X currently blaring from the speakers above my head. I began to turn, then panicked. So much for telling myself she couldn't hurt me.

The bar was suddenly too loud, the crush of people around me too much. My heart was pounding again, and my skin itched. I needed to vault the bar and get away. I needed…

"Breathe, Garrett." Jacki had her hands on my shoulders. "We got you. Okay? Just take a few deep breaths."

Jacki positioned her wide shoulders to give us both some space from the crush. Bex held their drinks now and looked concerned.

"I'm okay," I lied. "I'll be okay."

Well, that last one was slightly more accurate.

"Do you need me to take you outside?" Jacki asked.

Hmm. Did I? I inhaled the mingled scents of too many people, clashing colognes, beer, and fruity drinks. Then I exhaled. Slowly. Checked in with myself.

The sense of being overwhelmed was fading.

"No. I'm good. Thanks."

I looked at Bex and mouthed "Is she still here?"

Bex shook her head. It was as if a balloon deflated inside me, releasing all its tension. I exhaled again, for real this time.

If I'm prepared beforehand, I can mostly hold my own in an overstimulating environment, but sometimes one small thing will push me into overload.

Like seeing the woman who broke my heart and tried to take my livelihood away before I'd even gotten a toehold in the business.

Yeah. I hadn't heard she was back in town. Last I knew, she'd gone to Nashville to "take some of that country music money." Not a bad move for a person who turned out to be a shark. Not that that's fair to sharks. Sharks are actually not as bad as people make them out to be.

Jacki shook me gently. "Garrett. Come back. She's not here."

"Right." I smiled too brightly, and wiped my sweaty palms on my trousers.

Jacki had somehow angled me up against the bar without me realizing it, because the next thing I knew, Ace thumped my drinks down on the bar.

I handed over my card. She nodded without speaking and slid it across the reader on her little handheld machine. But before she handed it back, she speared me with a look.

"You're better than her, Garrett. Don't forget it."

Right. I nodded as if I believed her. And when it was just John, the dogs, and I, I did. But as soon as we were in a crowd like this? My sense of belonging faded, even though I was surrounded by friends.

"Thanks," I said, but Ace was already gone. Onto the next customer.

"Where's John?" Bex asked. "Should we get a table?"

"He's holding one for us," I pointed. "Over there."

Bex and Jacki took the drinks, for which I was grateful. No way could I press through the crowd to the table feeling the way I was and keep our drinks from sloshing overboard.

As I wove my way through the bright and glittering crowd, I couldn't help but wonder again:

What was Vyviane doing back? And why now?

CHAPTER 18
Marsha

THE DOG BED next to the fireplace was so warm. So fluffy. So cozy. Even when no fire was lit, like now, it was still one of my favorite spots.

Klaus snored softly next to me, then stopped. Paws twitching, he gave a soft woof as though onto prey. Probably a squirrel. Klaus hates squirrels. Or loves them, depending on what angle you look at the situation from. He hates squirrels because they come into our territory and yell at us. One in particular has it out for Klaus and likes to throw things at his long tan nose while clucking away.

But my theory is that if all the squirrels disappeared, Klaus would be bored. He likes a little excitement now and then. All corgis do. And an excuse to bark his head off?

Come on. That's just fun.

I squirmed closer to Klaus's back, ready to rest my eyes again, when I heard a noise.

It couldn't be Adam. The ghost was around, but he

generally didn't make noise. No. It was the front porch. Maybe Garrett and John were home?

I pricked up my ears and swiveled them toward the big front door.

It wasn't Garrett and John. Not their footfalls. Besides, they always murmured softly to each other when they came home late at night.

No. Someone was sneaking on the porch. That also ruled out possums and raccoons. Both of those animals thought they were sneaky but boy howdy, could they make a racket!

I rose and padded across the big, patterned carpet in the half dark living room. One small lamp burned on a side table, and a light was on in the kitchen, enough for my keen eyes to make out movement across the front window curtains where the fake flame porch light threw shadows.

And the shadow moving right now? Was human. And it wasn't a shape I recognized.

I growled.

"What's happening?" Klaus asked in a sleepy voice behind me.

"Intruder."

::Intruder?:: That was Adam's voice in my head. The ghost must have come in the room when I was distracted.

I kept my eyes on the shadow, then moved forward to inch the curtain aside.

::Let me.:: Adam twitched the curtain just enough for me to get behind it easily. Soon enough, my paws were on the dark wood windowsill.

I peered into the night. The flickering orange fake flame danced across the broad front porch. I saw nothing except the trees and street beyond. Everything was dark and quiet.

Then I heard a squeak. And another squeak. The squeaking formed a rhythm that I recognized. The double porch swing. It had been John's gift to Garrett a year ago. The men liked to sit on it some evenings, snuggled up, with Klaus and I at their feet.

I loved those nights.

But now? The intruder sat and swung, dainty feet dangling from the moving perch. Pale feet were enclosed in sparkly shoes. A dark coat covered her dress, and her face was white as the moon with a cloud of pale hair drifting over the darkness.

::Who is she?:: Adam asked.

Klaus shoved me over and placed his own paws on the windowsill.

"She's pretty."

"That doesn't matter!" I woofed. *"She's an intruder."*

"But..."

::Marsha is right, Klaus,:: Adam's voice backed me up in a low rumble. *::Strange people shouldn't just come sit on the porch late at night.::*

"Maybe she's a friend?" Klaus's voice was tentative. He was too soft hearted. Sometimes I wished he'd take a little of the anger he has at squirrels and channel it into more productive wariness.

But then he wouldn't be Klaus.

"Then why haven't we seen her here before?" I pointed out.

Klaus whined in frustration. He does that when he knows I'm right but doesn't want to admit it.

::I'm going out,:: Adam said.

We both turned our heads to stare at the ghost. I think my jaw dropped.

"You can do that?" Klaus squeaked.

The ghost's face looked determined. At least, what I could see of it between his leather cap and that enormous mustache. He squared his shoulders beneath his leather vest and walked toward the front door.

Passing halfway through it, he got stuck. One boot in the house, one boot somewhere on the front mat, I guess. I couldn't see it through the slab of wood.

Adam cursed, using a colorful phrase I didn't recognize, but there was no mistaking the intent. Believe me, I've been around humans long enough to tell what words are considered no-nos, just by a person's tone of voice.

He yanked himself back into the house, stumbling back almost to the big carved newel post.

We ran to him.

"Adam!" Klaus barked, *"are you okay?"*

The ghost shook his head as if confused, then braced himself on the newel post, one hand on his chest.

::Fine. I'll be fine. That was just… really, really weird.::

He stared at the door, face a mixture of disgust and longing. For the first time, I wondered what it would be like to not be able to leave a place. Especially when you were used to wandering the neighborhoods, sniffing out good things, whenever you pleased.

I trotted over and licked his hand. My tongue went halfway through his ice-cold hand. Which was weird. And gross. And a little disturbing.

But it got half a smile from him, which made it worth it.

The rhythmic squeaking on the front porch stopped.

I ran to the cracked curtain again, barking my head off. Klaus barked wildly at my feet.

The person on the porch looked at me, eyes wide with fear. I put all the fierceness in my body into my barks, lips curling back, teeth bared.

Then something astonishing happened. The person's face changed. She smiled at me!

And then she blew me a kiss!

How dare she?

I barked and growled with all my might, claws scratching at the window, Klaus barking frantically below me.

The person whirled, cloud of blonde hair flying around her shoulders. It was as if something in the street had startled her. She dropped something on the porch with a small thunk, then ran, sparkly shoes catching the light until they disappeared.

Klaus and I barked and barked, chasing the strange person on her way.

Then Garrett rushed up the porch steps, looking worried.

"Marsha?" I heard him say through the glass. "Klaus?"

John rushed up the steps in his high heeled shoes, the kind that click on the bare floors like my claws. He had his made-up face on, which was different from his ordinary face. But unlike the intruder, I would recognize John no matter what he wore, or how much makeup he caked over his skin.

Soon enough, the front door was opened and Garrett rushed inside, smelling slightly of alcohol and other people's perfume. He crouched down, and Klaus and I rushed him, barking excitedly.

"There was an intruder!" I barked.

"On the porch!" Klaus woofed.

"An intruder!"

"On the porch!"

"And they dropped something!"

"On the porch!"

Garrett looked confused. "What has gotten into you two? Was there an opossum outside or something? We've talked about that. Possums are good friends. They eat nasty bugs that we don't want around."

"Not a possum," I growled softly.

"An intruder!" Klaus barked happily, loving the excitement. See what I mean about the squirrels? Klaus lives for this stuff.

::The dogs are right,:: Adam said. *::Someone was on the porch.::*

Garrett looked around, as if he'd heard something. That was interesting. Both John and Garrett knew the ghost lived with us, of course, or had, since Klaus and I had dug out the boxes filled with Adam's things. But I didn't think they could hear him.

"Adam?" Garrett asked. "Are you there?"

Then he turned back to us. "Is that why you're barking?"

John stepped into the house. Where had he been?

"Babe. They aren't barking at the ghost."

He held something out in his hands.

"This was on the porch. Someone was here."

CHAPTER 19

Garrett

I FROZE IN MY CROUCH, surrounded by my two dogs, staring up at the man I loved. His painted face looked serious, and I didn't want to see what he held in his hands.

I couldn't say why, I just knew I wasn't going to like it. I patted the dogs on their fuzzy little heads and rose, eyes never leaving John's beautiful face, painted with smoky eye shadow and tangerine lipstick, cheekbones high-lighted with enough sparkle to catch the porch light coming in through the front door.

Maybe if I didn't look, whatever was in his hands would go away.

"Babe." He held out a hand and gently touched the sleeve of my blazer. The blazer I had put on only hours ago, feeling so dapper next to my beautiful date, heading to the nightclub to see our friends, and pick up any gossip that might point us to Saschi's killer.

And then Vyviane appeared, ruining it all. I was so out of it, very little information gathering had gotten done, despite John and I questioning our friends. And I never had seen Enrico. Wouldn't have been able to question him coherently if I had. John and I drank our one drink, but he could tell something was off and brought me home.

I was thankful Bex and Jacki didn't say anything to John. I'd tell him in my own time, and a crowded nightclub was not the place to get into it.

But those same friends were right. I shouldn't let my ex get to me. But I also couldn't help but wonder why she was back. And when I would run into her again.

John held out a slender object with a mouthpiece on one end, like the kind you see on cheap cigars.

"A vape pen?" I asked.

He nodded. "Someone was definitely here. And look, there's lipstick around the edges."

"Let me turn on more lights."

I moved past a draught and shivered. Was something wrong with the insulation? Or was it the ghost?

I still wasn't used to living with a ghost, but so far, he was pretty low impact.

Snapping on a Mission style lamp with a glass shade in triangle patterns of orange and cream, I turned back to my love. The dogs both looked up at John. Klaus whined, and Marsha pawed the carpet and sniffed at the air. This all felt so strange.

Every muscle in my body was tense. I sighed, forcing my shoulders down from around my ears.

"I can't deal with anything else tonight," I said.

John tilted his head at me, a sympathetic look on his face. "I'm sorry, babe."

He held the vape pen between two fingers, clutching it

delicately at the end opposite the mouthpiece. Catching me looking at it, he grimaced.

"I really shouldn't have touched this," he said. "Can you get a plastic bag from the kitchen?"

I nodded and rushed into the kitchen, flipping on a light switch as I went. Klaus and Marsha followed, watching carefully in case I decided they deserved a snack. And if they had scared off whoever left the vape pen on the porch, maybe they would get one.

But right now, I was slamming open kitchen drawers, as if I had forgotten where everything was.

"Babe. It's in the drawer to the left of the sink."

I stopped my frantic search, hands dropping to my sides. My breath was coming hard and fast, and I felt a meltdown coming on.

Forcing myself to slow down, I took in a long, slow breath, walked to the sink, opened the drawer, and pulled out a plastic bag.

By the time I turned to hand it to John, I was calmer. Not calm, but calmer.

He dropped the vape pen into the open bag. I sealed it and set it on the narrow island, then stepped into his arms. He'd kicked off those damn heels at the doorway, so I fit comfortably against his chest.

"Dang. Forgot to take off my shoes."

All I'd been able to think about was calming the dogs down.

I felt John laugh against me. "I think I can forgive you. But just this once. Don't make a habit of it."

I looked up into his beautiful face and pulled him down into a gentle kiss, which left a sticky film of lipstick on me. I pulled out a handkerchief and wiped it off.

"Getting rid of the evidence so soon?" he asked.

I gave him a playful push. He knows I hate the feel of lipstick. As a matter of fact, I hate anything on my face and only wear lotion or sunscreen out of necessity.

Marsha barked. *"We saw a woman!"*

"With blonde hair!" Klaus joined in.

John and I looked down at the two adorable corgis, Marsha with her black head and tri-colored markings and Klaus with his pale tannish-red and white. Both their tails wagged encouragingly.

"Don't you wish we could understand what they're saying?" John asked.

"I think they want a treat and considering that they scared off the person we saw running down the block, they deserve one."

I headed for the treat canister on the white quartz countertop and pulled out two small nibbles.

Klaus and Marsha waited patiently.

"You were very good to protect the house," I said, feeding one to Marsha and the other to Klaus. They chomped the treats down, then pawed for more.

"That's enough, you two," John said. "It's too late to eat. And I need to get out of this dress."

I looked down at the plastic bag and the wand of the vape pen. Then I looked closer.

"Do you recognize that lipstick?" I asked.

John peered down at the pen, paused a moment, then shook his head.

"Do you?" he asked.

"Maybe. I don't know."

All of the overwhelm from the evening rushed back, causing my stomach to clench. The noise. The music. The crush of people. And seeing Vyviane. I pressed my hands to my ears as if I could block it all out.

John pulled me into his arms again. "Sshhh. Just breathe. You're home now. We're going upstairs. You're going to put on your pajamas and I'm going to get this goop off my face. Then you're going to tell me what's going on."

I nodded, then clapped my hands. "Marsha, Klaus, time for bed."

The corgis led the way out of the kitchen and began their ascent up the staircase. I paused to lock the front door and take my shoes off, setting them neatly in the rack as John turned the lights off downstairs, leaving only the muted LED nightlights glowing on the stairs.

He followed me up. Klaus and Marsha sniffed around the closet doors.

"Think they see the ghost?" I asked.

"Probably. I felt a cold spot downstairs and it didn't seem like a draft."

He slipped out of his dress and sat on the edge of the bed to roll down his stockings. I opened the closet and hung my blazer neatly next to my other sports coats and suits. I took off my bow tie and placed it carefully in the drawer with the other ties and pocket squares, then threw my white dress shirt in the hamper.

"You want to tell me what's going on?"

John stood in the closet doorway, wrapped in a long, goldenrod-colored silk robe with peony flowers splashed across the bottom. He was wiping at his face with a damp cloth, leaving streaks of makeup smeared across his skin.

I pulled a set of burgundy pajamas from a drawer and slipped them on, motioning him back to the bathroom across the hallway. Hundred-year-old homes aren't big on en-suite bathrooms. John turned in a swirl of silk. I shoved my feet into slippers and followed him into the brightly lit room, with its green and black tiles and matching pedestal sinks.

John rinsed the cloth and started back in on cleaning his face.

I leaned in the doorway.

"Vyviane was at the bar."

He dropped the washcloth and whirled.

"That's why you were freaked out? I thought it was just the stress of the club after your day. And you didn't tell me?"

I shrugged. "It was too noisy to get into it. I was already feeling overwhelmed. Besides, we were there to pump people for clues about Saschi, not to watch me have a meltdown."

He turned back to his ablutions, but I could tell he was upset.

"Hey," I said gently, "Ace and Jacki had my back. We didn't even talk. By the time I got our drinks, she was gone."

He leaned on the sink, staring at me in the mirror.

"You still should have told me."

I held up a hand. "You're right. I should have. I apologize."

He gave the washcloth a final rinse and turned his face this way and that, making sure his skin was clean. Satisfied, he opened the medicine cabinet and started putting on his various serums and unguents. It's a process I didn't quite understand, but it made him happy, so who am I to judge?

I watched my beautiful partner for a while, turning the night's events over in my head. We'd gotten some information, but nothing I would exactly call a clue. I hoped that sleeping on it would jog some nuggets loose from the swirl of my mind. But for now? There was one important piece of information I needed to share with John.

"I think that's Vyviane's lipstick on the vape pen. I think she was the person we saw running away."

CHAPTER 20

Marsha

I WAS GRUMPY.

We hadn't gotten enough sleep last night, what with the intruder, plus John and Garrett coming home late. Garrett seemed out of sorts, too, and John was a little grumpy but trying to hide it, which meant he was worried about something, probably Garrett.

It was a "go with Garrett to the shop" day. I hoped to get in several good naps there.

Our collars jingled as Klaus and I trotted along the sidewalk. It had rained at some point early in the morning, so the flowers and bushes were damp and smelled good. I was hoping to stop by Bruiser's before we headed to the store, but with Garrett's mood, I couldn't tell what would happen.

Humans. They are so temperamental. We corgis are much more reasonable. We bark when something is wrong. We eat. We sleep. We play. We wag our tails and wiggle our butts.

That's it. No problem. None of this hiding our feelings

or getting stressed about things that we can't fix. Either we love you to death or we growl. Simple. Humans seem to have a lot of in between. Talk about confusing: Sometimes they love and growl at the same time.

What kind of sense does that make?

We rounded the corner onto Pride Street, walking under the canopy of the big trees. And… yes! There was Bruiser!

I barked a greeting. He barked back. Then Klaus joined in. We looked at each other, I gave Klaus the signal, and we both put on speed, tugging at our leashes in our hurry to greet our friend.

"Marsha P. Johnson! Klaus Nomi! Slow down!"

Garrett tried to pull us back to heel, but I was having none of it. I wanted a biscuit, and I wanted to see if Bruiser had any news. The humans think they know everything, but frankly, they hadn't gotten very far with Saschi's death.

It was clear they needed all the canine assistance we could offer.

Bruiser wagged his stump of a tail, wiggling from side to side with a great amount of enthusiasm bordering on violence. Bruiser is a very expressive dog. Passionate, even. And heck if he wasn't even more excited to see us than usual.

"Bruiser!" Klaus barked, tugging harder at his leash.

"Klaus! Marsha! I was hoping you would come today!"

Well, that was interesting. I woofed a greeting but didn't say anything else. There would be time for questions in a moment. The humans didn't like it when we barked too much inside. I don't know why. Humans are always yapping their heads off, indoors and out. But dogs? Oh no. We had to stay quiet indoors or get shushed.

The café was fairly quiet. Just a few humans sitting at tables inside, working at laptops or reading. One person was knitting near a window, and let me tell you, that ball of blue yarn looked very tempting. But I'd learned the hard way that humans don't consider balls of yarn toys.

So why do they make them ball shaped?

Bruiser sidled up to my shoulder and mumbled something.

"What's that?" I woofed as softly as I could.

"A human came in, asking about Garrett. Pretending like she knew him. But I didn't trust her."

I looked at Bruiser's smashed-in face and the slender line of drool dangling off the side of his mouth. His watery eyes seemed concerned.

"Why didn't you trust her?"

"She smelled wrong. Like she was lying. And she sat outside for a while, with one of those disgusting vapor pens that humans think aren't noxious, but really are. I hate those things."

"Marsha P? Do you want a cookie?"

I startled. Garrett looked down at me, blinking through his glasses.

What a question. Of course, I wanted a cookie. I woofed a solid *"yes!"* and swished my beautiful tail for emphasis. Bruiser talking about that human disturbed me, but I felt much less grumpy now. Cookies always make things better.

Then I heard Bex talking to Garrett and pricked up my ears.

"A certain person is back in town. And asking about you."

"Really? She was here?"

I looked up at the counter where Garrett was paying. The dog cookies were sitting. Right. There. I got onto my hind legs and leaned against the front of the counter, lifting my nose as high as I could. If I stretched just a little bit more, I could almost reach the closest cookie.

"Marsha P. Johnson! What are you doing?"

I looked up at Garrett and blinked, then smiled my biggest smile and swished my tail again.

As I suspected would happen, his face broke into a grin.

"Okay. Okay. You may have your cookie now. But don't get crumbs on the floor!"

As if I would waste one morsel of one of Jacki's homemade cookies.

Garrett handed me my treat, then offered treats to Klaus and Bruiser, too. I immediately gripped it in my teeth and raced toward the door, leash trailing. Klaus and Bruiser were hot on my heels.

"Hey!" Garrett shouted.

I didn't bother stopping. Once Garrett realized we were just out front, he'd deal. I pulled up at the tables outside the café and dove beneath the closest one to munch my cookie.

Once our treats were done, it was time to get down to business.

"*So,*" I asked Bruiser, who was licking his substantial chops, "*what else did you find out?*"

"*When she was out here with her disgusting vapor pen, I heard her on the phone with someone.*"

Both Klaus and I swiveled our ears to Bruiser and leaned closer.

"She said she wanted Garrett back. Something about him being much more intriguing now that he was a full-fledged man." Bruiser furrowed the already deep wrinkles in his brow. *"But I don't understand what that means."*

"Human stuff," I said, even though I didn't understand, either. *"Garrett is Garrett, and people are just weird. Go on."*

"Ain't that the truth?" Bruiser replied, but then fell into silence. Or as silent as a wheezing bulldog can be.

I sat at attention, waiting for the bulldog to finish. Klaus rested his snout on his paws, lazy dog.

"Let me see." Bruiser gazed across the street, where Petunia the florist was setting out a sign announcing the day's specials. Though what was so special about another bunch of flowers, I wasn't sure. The only specials I care about are treats.

"She also called that waiter person a bad name and said, 'her blackmailing days are over, I guess.'"

"That doesn't sound too good," Klaus murmured.

No. It didn't. It didn't sound too good at all.

CHAPTER 21

Garrett

MY FIRST-IN-LINE CLIENT, Tomaso, was waiting for me when the dogs and I arrived. He tapped his leather shoe against the sidewalk and checked the fancy silver watch around his burly wrist. His hair was perfectly groomed in a dark, glossy sweep off his high forehead. His brown eyes snapped with impatience.

Tomaso might dress like the high-end investor he now was, but he couldn't erase the boxer he used to be, once upon a time. He made his money and got out before it ruined his good looks. I'm not kidding. That's his actual story.

He has one little scar above his right eye, but that just makes him more intriguing. At least, he thinks so.

"Tomaso! Thank you so much for waiting. I got held up."

"Held up at the café, it looks like." He sniffed, gesturing toward my coffee cup with his chin. "I don't suppose you brought me any?"

As it was clear there was only one cup in my hand and the dog leashes in the other, I didn't comment, just unlocked the door.

Once inside, I flipped on the lights, unhooked the corgis from their leashes, and turned my brightest smile on my already disgruntled customer.

"May I put the kettle on? I can offer you tea or French press coffee."

He hmphed. "No. Let's just get on with this."

Okay. Most clients were excited about using my services. Happy, even. Sometimes I had to talk a person down from their nerves, and people got upset at delays or overages, but I'd never had someone surly before the project really began before.

"All right!" I said in my brightest voice. "Shall we sit?"

I was determined that this project go well. A few of the windowsills in our hundred-and-ten-year-old Craftsman needed repairing, and we should likely replace the roof soon.

Or put up solar. We kept debating which should come first in the budget.

I grabbed my notebook and large tablet and led Tomaso to my favorite sofa and chairs grouping. The same set that had hosted Saschi's grieving friends. The dogs were already settled on their big bed close by.

Flipping my notebook open, I powered up the tablet and soon had his mood board up and ready on a split screen with his main floor plans.

"I was thinking we should remove this pony wall with the breakfast bar and restore the original cased opening. The rooms will flow much better that way." And remain true to the original architecture of his classic old four-square home. Who wanted open concept, anyway? Its days are waning, mark my words.

When I glanced up at Tomaso, he was staring out the window, not looking at my designs at all.

"Tomaso? What do you think?"

I tapped the tablet with my stylus, pointing out the offending breakfast bar.

He shook his head and leaned forward, elbows braced on his black gabardine clad knees. Uh oh. Was he going to give me trouble? It was unfortunately highly likely.

"What did Saschi tell you?" His voice was a growl, but there was no real heat in it. As a matter of fact, despite the angry scowl on his handsome face, I would say that Tomaso was scared. Sweat dotted his upper lip, despite the temperate spring weather, and his hand lifted as if to rake itself through that perfect sweep of hair.

He caught himself. That sort of vanity took real discipline, but I guess an ex-boxer would have that in spades.

"Tell me? Tell me what?" I set the tablet down on my lap. Things were about to get interesting. Marsha pricked up her big fuzzy ears but kept her head down. Waiting. Klaus snored. I swear Marsha looked disgusted at his sloth.

I stifled a grin and waited for Tomaso to answer.

What I got was another scowl.

"I know you liked that creature." His voice dripped with disdain. "Though why, I cannot say."

"Everyone liked Saschi," I said, though it had become quite clear that was not the case. "What did they do to piss you off?"

He burst up from his seat and began to pace behind the long, blue velvet sofa.

"What did they do? What did they do?" He raked his hands through his hair for real. Amazingly, his fingers ran all the way through. I thought for sure they'd get caught up in all the hair product he wore up there. Guess that's the difference between my drugstore stuff and the high-end products that cost more than I make in a day. Maybe they really are worth it.

"That vile creature was blackmailing me!"

"Whoa," I said, holding out my hands. "That's a pretty strong accusation!"

And one that was coming from too many quarters.

"As if you didn't know!" Tomaso's upper lip curled into a snarl.

Marsha barked. I sshhed her, not wanting to interrupt his rant. It was clear he was about to get to the good stuff.

She grumbled but settled back down on the bed. I noticed her eyes were trained on Tomaso now, and her ear tips practically vibrated. Even Klaus had woken up and was watching.

"I'm sorry, Tomaso, but I didn't. To me, Saschi was just a fun waiter at my favorite sushi place. Sure, they liked to gossip, but who in this community doesn't? It didn't ever feel malicious to me."

The wind seemed to leave him, and he dropped to the couch as if deflated. Then he carefully reset that sweep of hair with his hands. Impressive. How in the heck he did that with no comb or mirror was practically a gay miracle. Choirs of drag queens were singing somewhere, I was sure of it.

"So, you never heard anything about me?"

"I didn't." Well, except that he was wealthy, vain, and a little bit selfish in bed. Some folks speculated on how exactly he made his money these days, but I always chalked that up to sour grapes and not understanding finance.

Not that I blame people, mind you. When the rich get richer and the poor get poorer, it's hard to not notice the system is rigged. But a rigged system didn't mean Tomaso was cheating. At least, not any more than any other wealthy person.

But looking at him now, I wasn't so sure it was unscrupulous financial projects he was talking about.

The way he was blotting his upper lip pointed to something a lot closer to home.

"Are you in trouble?" I kept my voice soft and calm, the way I would talk to a spooked dog.

When he looked up at me, I saw that he was crying and his face was flushed. The little white scar stood out in relief above his eye.

"I'm about to lose everything that matters. All because of one stupid thing. One stupid thing I'll regret to the end of my days."

He stood again, dabbed at his face, tucked his damp handkerchief back into his jacket pocket. Then he shot his cuffs, and gave me a crisp nod, as if we'd had a satisfactory meeting that was now over.

I stood, too. "Don't you want to go over my designs?"

My words felt feeble, but they were the only ones that occurred to me. I'm not always super quick on my feet.

He waved a hand at the notebook and tablet, both abandoned on the coffee table.

"I'm sure they're all fine." He smiled a bright, fake, smile. "I trust you, Garrett."

He held out a hand and shook mine firmly, then, looking me dead in the eyes, he repeated himself.

"I trust you."

Why did those three little words sound like a warning?

CHAPTER 22

Adam

NOW THAT I'D been awakened from whatever weird twilight state I'd been in, I was bored.

Yeah, ghosts can get bored. You float around a house when everyone is at work and you have nothing to do. Sounds restful, you say? Yeah. For a day or two, maybe. But after that? See how long you like it.

I could hear John typing away in his office. A slender, handsome, Asian man, he was the type I would always admire but never hook up with. I preferred my men with a bit more heft to them, if you know what I mean. But there was no denying John is beautiful.

Garrett is lovely in his own way, too, but he's even smaller than John. Almost delicate, with his peaches and cream skin and his silly bow ties and tweedy jackets. Garrett dresses like a college professor from 1958.

The dogs were with him at his store, which left me at loose ends. I'd already run through my gamut of experiments. How large an object could I lift? How much weight could I push?

Turns out, not much, but also just enough.

Marsha had shown me a computer in the spare bedroom where Garrett worked on designs sometimes. It didn't have a password, and if I concentrated, I could use just enough force to push the keys.

These new computers were a marvel. They were sleek and chrome or black, not the heavy, clunky slabs of grayish tan plastic that always smelled like they were burning if you used them for more than an hour.

Not that I had a computer myself, back in the day. No need for one. But one of my housemates was into all that techy stuff, so I knew enough.

We didn't have the World Wide Web back then, though. That was a new thing. Seemed useful. Marsha tried to explain it to me, but I gleaned more information from listening to John talk about his research to Garrett. The man almost never goes to the library. To look things up, he just uses what he calls his "business and research computer."

Astounding. The man has two computers. One for writing, and one for business. And from the looks of things, he's not even that rich. I mean, the household doesn't want for food, that's for sure, but they're not rolling in the dough, either.

At any rate, here I am, alone in front of Garrett's computer. I want to find out more about these vape pens and what might have killed the waiter.

I also wanted to find out more about the person on the front stoop the night before. I saw her out there, and she definitely looked up to no good.

The thing I can't figure out?

If the dogs hadn't scared her off before the men got home, what would she have done?

And was she capable of murder?

More people are than we sometimes like to think.

CHAPTER 23

Garrett

MARSHA WHINED IN CONCERN, pawing at my leg as Klaus sniffed at the piece of paper held carefully between my fingertips.

I'd been in the back room, making a cup of tea, when I heard the bell chime. But in the few seconds it took me to flip aside the curtain and step back into the main part of the store, the chimes rang a second time, and whoever had entered had left again.

But there was this piece of paper. An ugly thing, with letters cut out from the free weekly rag the local business association puts out. I advertise in the thing myself, just to support the LGBTQ Business Association, or Queer BA as some of us call it, but I don't think I've ever gotten a customer from the thing.

"Stop your snooping or your dog is dead," it read.

Well, someone knew how to hit me where it hurt. But unlike seeing Vyviane, instead of sending me into a spiral of overwhelm, this just made me mad. So I had texted John, and made myself a cup of tea.

The dogs and I were back at the front counter now, waiting for him to arrive. I tapped a pen on the counter and stared down at the ugly note, then glanced at the dogs. Klaus was sleeping, but Marsha stared up at me, as if she could sense something was up. She always knew, that one. Sometimes I think she's a doggy psychic.

Marsha yipped at me.

"Don't worry, Marsha. I won't let anyone touch you. You either, Klaus Nomi."

The bells chimed. I looked up, heart racing, only to relax. It was John, jeans and T-shirt rumpled, one shoelace untied, and his beautiful face creased in concern. He rushed to my side.

"Are you okay? What happened? You said there was a note?"

I jabbed a finger toward where it crouched on the counter. "Don't touch it."

He gave me one of his *I'm a mystery and thriller writer, don't you think I know that?* looks, but didn't say anything. I was thankful for that. Couples need to know when to cut each other some slack, and John knows all the signs when I'm nearing overload.

And I was. Again.

He leaned over the paper. "Holy smokes. You and Marsha have struck a nerve."

I nodded, then carefully slid the paper into a file folder using the edge of a pen cap. I then locked it in a file drawer behind the counter. Not super secure, but it would have to do for now.

"Come into the back? I made myself a cup of tea, but never got to drink it."

John flipped the sign to closed and locked the door. I

thought about objecting, but he was right. I needed an actual break to deal with whatever this was.

"Would you put up the Back in Fifteen sign?"

He raised an eyebrow at that, but I had to tell my customers something. I couldn't just close with no explanation. I'd make us tea and we could come back out on the chance that anyone stopped by.

Marsha followed us into the back room, nosy girl, leaving Klaus to whatever dreams made his paws twitch.

"Who have you been talking with?" John asked, as I clicked the electric kettle on and dumped my cold tea in the tiny break room sink. I got him a mug and plopped tea bags into two mugs. Mint for John, and a black breakfast tea for me. John only drank caffeine in coffee form, first thing in the morning. After that, he was a bit of a "my body is a temple" kind of guy. Hence his lean muscles and all that.

Don't get me wrong, I appreciate his muscles. I'm just glad he also likes my soft, pale belly, because it isn't going anywhere.

"Well, we spoke with a few people the other night at Enrico's. And then there's Bex and Jacki. Yarrow. And Ron. And this morning? Tomaso came in for his appointment and was acting really weird."

"Weird how?"

John was crouched down, scratching Marsha's chin.

I poured the boiling water into the waiting mugs.

"Well, he was all sweaty and nervous, and I swear he threatened me before he left."

John's chin jerked up and he looked at me, mouth set in a line, lips almost disappearing the way they only did when he was angry.

"Threatened you how?"

I threw the teabags in the compost, and added some coconut creamer to my tea, bringing John his mug. He stood, his fingers brushing mine for a moment. The slight touch was his way of telling me he was with me, even though he was pissed off.

"It was more his tone than his words, if you know what I mean. He said, 'I trust you,' twice. Like, with emphasis."

"As if he was telling you he trusted you to keep your mouth shut?"

"That was it exactly. That was the threat. But I have no idea what I need to keep my mouth shut *about*. Come on, let's go sit out front so I can keep an eye on the store while we talk."

"*I didn't like him,*" Marsha barked.

"No. No treats for you, Marsha P. Johnson," John said.

"She's been very talky lately," I said, swishing the curtain back.

As if she heard me, Marsha raced to the front of the store, growling and barking at something in one of the front windows. Klaus woke up with a yelp.

"What is going on?" John asked.

I stepped very carefully toward the front windows. I couldn't make myself go any faster. It was almost as if I didn't want to see what was there.

And I was right. Dangling just outside, flapping in the spring breeze, was an upside-down miniature Pride flag. And hanging from that? A small stuffed animal, with a rope around its neck.

It looked an awful lot like a corgi.

CHAPTER 24

Marsha

I COULDN'T BELIEVE IT. Who would do such a thing?

"Is that me?" Klaus asked, voice trembling with fear.

It sure looked like Klaus, though without his nice tail, but that was probably just because it was the only stuffed corgi toy the human could find. Between this and the note Garrett found, it was pretty clear someone was targeting *me*, Marsha P. Johnson.

But why? Did that mean I was close to solving the case?

I stared up at the monstrosity, then barked in frustration. I saw John outside the window, carefully taking the thing down. Klaus and I ran to meet him at the door.

He dangled the thing from a long string.

"They tied it to the awning."

I sniffed. It smelled weird, but I couldn't quite place it. And where had I smelled that before? It was kind of harsh, making my nose tingle, and not in a good way.

"It smells like cleaning supplies!" I barked.

Klaus shoved me aside to sniff himself. *"You're right. But not the kind Garrett and John use."*

I looked at my friend's fuzzy tan face. He blinked.

"Who has cleaning supplies that smell like this?" I asked.

He swiveled his ears and furrowed his brow, but I could tell he hadn't come up with anything.

John and Garrett were getting a bag to put the toy into when I realized where I'd smelled it.

"Bruiser's," I said, feeling both pleased and alarmed. Pleased that I'd figured it out, but alarmed that someone we were friends with might wish us harm.

"Fred's" Klaus barked. *"I've smelled it at Fred and Ron's!"*

Oh no. Klaus was right. Both Bruiser's Best Beans and Bones, Dogs, and Harmony smelled a little bit like the toy.

"Maybe it doesn't mean anything," I barked. *"Maybe the toy smells like that because they bought it at Fred and Ron's."*

Klaus looked at me with big, sad eyes. Neither of us believed it.

"Our toys never smell like that," Klaus pointed out.

"Yeah." I sighed, then clicked my way to Garrett's favorite big sofa, where he and John sat talking.

"The toy smells like Bruiser's and Fred's," I barked.

John reached out a hand and I walked under it. I'm not one to refuse a head scratching, even though I had impor-tant things to convey.

"Quiet, girl. We're trying to think," he said.

As if I wasn't helping. Humans! They are so frustrating sometimes!

"Do you think it came from Bones, Dogs, and Harmo-ny?" Garrett asked.

Finally! Someone was listening to me.

"Could be," John said. "You don't think Ron had anything to do with this, though? Do you?"

Garrett shook his head. "I can't imagine it. But then, I can't imagine anyone wanting to kill Saschi, either. Except maybe Tomaso. But even then, a man like that wouldn't want to get his hands dirty, would he?"

John sipped his tea. I plopped my butt down on the rug, listening. Maybe I could pick up some more clues.

"He could hire someone," John said.

That was reasonable. Humans hired other humans for all sorts of things. Why not killing? Dogs were more honest. If we smelled a rat, we'd shake it to death ourselves as soon as we saw it.

"*What do you think, Klaus?*" I asked. Klaus wasn't the quickest thinker, but sometimes that meant he noticed things I missed.

He chewed an old rawhide knot, thoughtfully.

"*I think Ron is a very good person. And Fred is too old to do any harm. Bruiser looks tough, but that dog is even scared of bees. How could he hurt a human, or another dog?*"

Good points.

"*How about Yarrow? Or Tomaso?*"

Klaus looked at me, his brown eyes sad.

"*I think both of them are hiding something.*"

But was that enough to kill over?

I started to say something, but then Klaus continued his out loud ruminations.

"*It could be someone Saschi worked with, too. We don't know anything about the restaurant, but if Saschi died there, it could be a human who worked with them.*"

"John! Garrett!" I barked. "*We didn't question anyone at the restaurant!*"

"Shhhh, Marsha P!" John admonished, standing up. "I'd better take these two for a walk, or you'll never get any peace. I wonder what's gotten into her?"

Garrett was looking down at me. "Sometimes I swear Marsha knows things. You think we should get one of those pet communication boards?"

"With the buttons? Heck no. We'll never get her to shut up, then!"

How rude! Those buttons sounded interesting, though. If I could train John and Garrett to use them, maybe they'd finally listen to me. I mean, Adam understands us just fine, why can't Garrett and John?

"Come on, you two. Walkies!"

"We're going out?" Klaus sounded disgruntled at the thought. *"Is it still raining?"*

"It stopped. Maybe we can drag John back to the restaurant and find more clues! Or stop by and talk to Fred or Bruiser."

John clipped our leashes to our harnesses, kissed Garrett goodbye, and soon we were out the door and trotting in the fresh spring air.

I tugged John toward Bruiser's, but he was having none of it.

"Oh no, you don't. No cookies for you! We're just going for a nice walk, okay?"

Sigh. There were clues to gather, and a case to solve, and John wanted a walk.

Humans. If it weren't for the head skritches, and food, and warm cozy beds? I wouldn't put up with them at all.

CHAPTER 25
Garrett

WE WERE BACK at the sushi restaurant, shaded by a big elm tree, tiny cups of tea steaming in front of us. It was weird being here with no Saschi to take our order.

"I don't know why we're here," John groused. "We have plenty of good food at home, including a chicken that needs roasting before it goes bad."

I looked around the courtyard to make sure no one was listening. An elderly lesbian couple traded nigiri two tables over. They were the sort of couple I aspired to be, clearly still very much in love after who knows how many years together. A young man and woman seemed to be having a snit to our left. Uh, oh. But at least trouble in paradise meant they wouldn't care what John and I were talking about. A burst of laughter from across the street drew my attention. It was a group of men flirting with each other outside Axle's bar.

I smiled, then remembered why I was looking around in the first place.

I leaned across the table, where John was frowning

over his menu. "We are here because I haven't had time to question the staff. What if one of them killed Saschi?"

"Garrett, don't you think we should leave this to someone with more authority?"

He reached across the table and took my hand. "That note, and the stuffed toy worry me. I don't want you or the furballs in danger."

I shook my head. "We're already in danger, John. And Saschi was our friend." Sort of. But Saschi was at very least a person we both liked, who made up part of the fabric of our little village-in-a-city. I realized I'd come to rely on those ordinary interactions with people I didn't know well. Goodwill was what stitched Pride Street together, keeping us safe and happy.

We all had each other's best interests in heart. At least, I used to think so. But clearly someone wished Saschi very, very ill. And if Saschi really had been blackmailing someone? Well, that was motive enough for murder, wasn't it?

"John! Garrett!" The owner of How We Roll approached, a water jug in hand.

Because of the upset of seeing Vyviane, I'd never gotten a chance to talk with him at Enrico's.

I pasted a smile on my face. Daniel was a nice guy but tried a bit too hard, if you know what I mean. He tried to bond with John over being Asian, which didn't go over too well. John and Daniel were polar opposites.

"He's so fake," John had complained to me more than once.

"Maybe he has social anxiety," I would always reply. I mean, I'm pretty sympathetic to that, and to other brain and personality weirdness. John's brain is as normal as they come—except for the blowing things up and killing people on the page thing—so he doesn't quite get it. He loves me, though, so that's what matters.

"We have special tempura tonight," Daniel said, looking at me. "Fresh eggplant along with the usual vegetables. Chef has been pressing the eggplants for hours."

He laughed a little too heartily, as though he'd just told us a hilarious joke. "I don't pretend to understand it, but she says it'll make them crisp up in the batter, and taste better, too. Who am I to argue?"

Who was he? Just one of the more successful business owners on Pride Street, but he knew we knew that.

"Sounds great," I said. "I'll take the veggie tempura and shrimp tempura, both."

"Dragon roll for me," John replied. "And the saba shioyaki."

"Great! Great!"

He smacked John on the back. John winced and gave Daniel a tight smile.

As he refilled our water glasses, I looked up into his handsome, pockmarked face. "Daniel, do you have any clue who might have wanted to hurt Saschi?"

Water sloshed over the side of my glass. I watched as fear, anger, and something else flashed across his face. Then he skinned those gleaming white teeth into a big, fake smile.

"Why would you ask that? Everyone loved Saschi! What a loss! Now, if you'll excuse me, I have to get your order in!" He bustled off, sloshing more water as he went, leaving tiny puddles on the concrete.

"Well, that was strange," I said.

"Daniel is always strange," John complained. "He thinks he's God's gift, or something."

"That's not what I meant. Did you see him? He looked afraid."

"Well, it's not every day one of your workers collapses in your kitchen."

I shook my head. "I'm going in there. I need to talk to him."

John gave me one of his *I hope you know what you're doing* looks but didn't say anything. He just popped an edamame in his mouth and waved me on my way.

I glanced under the table, where the two most innocent corgi faces stared back up at me.

"You two aren't fooling me for a minute. Stay with John, okay?"

Getting no response, I scurried past the planter boxes and into the cool dark of the restaurant, letting my eyes adjust. The place was half full, with people sitting at the big windows and on the stools that ringed the sushi bar. Daniel was just past that, at what I thought of as the waiter's station, refilling that pitcher of water. He was also engaged in what looked like an intense conversation with a waiter. She was someone I recognized but hadn't spoken to much because we always sat in Saschi's station.

I walked over, looking as if I was headed to the washrooms in back, but slowed down when I got to the station.

"Don't you dare say anything!" Daniel hissed. The waiter leaned as far away from him as she could in the cramped space.

"I-I won't. But Saschi…" She looked really distressed.

"Saschi got what was coming to them, didn't they? If

they had just kept their trap shut, they might be alive today. Let that be a lesson to you!"

The waiter caught me staring, and her eyes grew wide. Daniel whirled.

"You!" he said. "Were you eavesdropping?"

The waiter took the chance to rush off, shoving past me in her hurry to get away from her boss.

I gave him my most placid smile. At least, I hoped I did. My face doesn't always do what I want it to. John tells me I should never play poker.

"Just heading to the washroom. Too much tea!" I kept my voice chipper and moved past the station. Daniel grabbed my arm, hard.

"I've heard you've been snooping around. You'd better stop that before something bad happens."

I slowly turned my head and met his gaze. "Are you threatening me?"

He dropped my arm as if burned and pasted that fake smile back on his face. I squinted. The man had seriously bright veneers.

"No! No! Of course not," he said, in a complete about face. "We're all just worried. What happened to Saschi is a terrible thing, and I just don't want anyone else to get hurt."

Daniel picked up his water pitcher but didn't move.

"Of course. We don't want anyone else to get hurt," I replied, keeping my voice cool. "Which is why I'm doing my best to find out what happened to Saschi."

With that, I skirted by him and went to splash cold water on my face in the washroom.

I stared at my reflection in the bathroom mirror. My face was paler than usual, and my bow tie was askew. I dried my face on a rough paper towel and straightened my tie with shaking hands.

John was going to kill me when he found out what I said to Daniel. Taunting him was probably not the smartest thing I've ever done, but how else was I going to shake Saschi's killer loose?

My stomach growled, reminding me I hadn't eaten lunch and dinner was on the way.

As I walked back to John and the dogs, I saw my gluten-free tempura had already arrived at the table.

I just hoped it wasn't poisoned.

CHAPTER 26

Marsha

JOHN'S FOOT was shaking beneath the table, a sign that he was feeling anxious. I felt anxious, too, and wished Garrett had taken me with him into the restaurant. He shouldn't be around these people alone. No one knew who the killer was yet, and there were a lot of people involved that I didn't trust one bit.

Finally, Garrett pulled out his chair again, flopping heavily into the seat. I could hear him taking a big gulp of water.

What had happened that made him so thirsty?

"Took you long enough," John said. "I was about to send Marsha in to find you. Everything okay? You don't look so great."

"Thanks," Garrett said, in that tone of voice humans use when they mean the opposite of what they're saying.

"You know what I mean, babe. You look pale. As if you've seen a ghost or something."

"Daniel threatened me," Garrett said, keeping his voice

so low I was surprised John could hear. My corgi ears are superior, of course, and I heard him loud and clear.

"He what?" John hissed. I heard his chair scrape.

"John! Don't!"

John huffed but didn't get up.

"*Klaus,*" I woofed softly.

"*What?*"

"*I need to get inside the restaurant. Can you cover me?*"

Klaus looked around and sniffed the air. A low growl rumbled in his throat.

"*What are you growling for?*" That was not the response I expected from my usually agreeable friend.

"*Roses. I smell roses.*"

I sniffed the air, and sure enough, he was right.

We both inched our way out from beneath the table. John and Garrett were distracted by their food and barely noticed.

"Don't go anywhere, you two," John said, but he didn't sound suspicious. That was good.

"*Can you tell where the smell is coming from?*" I asked.

Klaus raised his little snoot and turned his head from right to left, and back again.

"*Over by the edge of the seating area. Under the cherry tree.*"

I looked past the sea of tables and legs, craning my neck to see. There was the blossoming tree. And underneath it were two people. Two people who had recently been in Garrett's shop!

"*It's Roderick and Princess Sparkle Toes!*" I barked. And they were kissing.

My bark alerted Garrett. "What the heck? That's weird."

"What's wrong?" John asked.

"Last time I saw Roderick and PST, they were arguing in my shop!" he hissed.

"Well, they look pretty cozy to me now. Maybe they're one of those couples who fight in order to make up?"

"It's not right!" I barked.

"They're not a couple," Garrett said. "At least, not that I've heard."

I strained at my leash.

"Marsha P! Stop tugging!" Garrett moved his chair more firmly beneath the table. The movement was all the chance I needed. I yanked hard and broke free. Soon I was dodging under tables, past shoes and boots. Someone yelled. Someone else dropped their beer. I heard it smash behind me and probably got some on my fur.

I didn't stop. No time to worry about beer-soaked fur right now. I had to get to Roderick and Princess Sparkle Toes. I had to find out which one smelled like roses.

"No, you don't!" The blonde woman from our front porch scooped me up, almost bumping heads with Sweetheart Digs, who was heading toward the restaurant.

I could smell roses, but the scent was confused by mint gum, spilled beer, and cigarettes. Plus, I couldn't tell which human the rose smell was coming from.

Daniel stepped up out of nowhere. "Marsha! If you can't behave, you have to leave!"

I struggled in the woman's arms, wriggling and kicking with all my might.

"That one belongs to Garrett and John," Sweetheart was saying. "I can take her back."

"Oh, that won't be necessary." The woman's voice was

cool as ice on a hot day. I shivered in her arms, then made another attempt to leap away. She held me tighter.

Drat!

"Klaus! Help!" I barked.

"What's going on?" That was Garrett's voice. I craned my head around. He stood a few paces away, hands loose at his sides as if he might need to rescue me. Or maybe like he was ready to punch someone, which was ridiculous. Garrett is not built for punching anything. John, now? He could punch whatever he wanted to, and from the look on his face, it seemed like he just might.

"Garrett!" The woman sounded delighted in that fake way humans sometimes have. Everything about her seemed fake. I growled and squirmed.

Now Garrett looked like he wanted to throw up. John stepped to his side.

"What, no welcome?" she said. "And aren't you going to introduce me?"

I kicked my back legs, scratching a bare arm, and felt the woman wince. But she didn't let go.

Drat, again.

"It's her!" Klaus barked. *"Garrett! John! It's the woman from the porch!"*

"Bite her, Klaus!" I yelled. *"Bite her!"*

I struggled and squirmed harder, but she only gripped tighter. What was her problem? Didn't she know to not hold a wild corgi in her arms?

I snapped at her white chin. She craned her head away.

"Now, now. Calm down, little pup. Before I squeeze the stuffing out of you," she hissed in my ear.

I kicked harder, scratching at her arms to get away. Klaus circled her legs, barking frantically.

As John reached forward to try to grab my front paws, the woman jerked me away.

"What do you think you're doing, lady?" John asked.

"Come on, Garrett," she cooed, stroking my head. I snapped again but couldn't reach her. "Aren't you going to introduce me to your boyfriend?"

Her voice mocked Garrett, I could tell. I decided I hated her, whoever she was. Garrett stood still as a stone. Still looking sick. But I felt like everyone was waiting for him to do something.

"Garrett!" I barked. *"Snap out of it!"*

CHAPTER 27

Garrett

THIS WAS MY WORST NIGHTMARE. I stood there in the courtyard beneath the shady elm trees, covered in a cold sweat. Vyviane stood in front of me, smiling like a barracuda, her arms around Marsha P. My stomach lurched. All that delicious gluten-free tempura suddenly turned sour.

I thought I was over her, but clearly, I wasn't. Seeing her in Enrico's? That was bad enough, but at least I was surrounded by friends and didn't have to talk to her.

But this. This was bad. She stood in front of me, that puff of blonde hair like a halo in the spring sunshine. Her perfect jeans and crisp white shirt. Those shoes with just the right amount of chunky heel.

Vyviane knew how to pull herself together. She knew how to flirt. How to flatter. How to ingratiate herself into situations and people's lives in order to get what she wanted.

And looking at her, I realized I wasn't over Vyviane at all.

Oh, I didn't love her anymore. No, I loathed her. But some part of her could still control me.

I remembered the bitter taste of shame as she humiliated me in front of my friends. I remembered the way she berated me in private. The way she tried to tease me out of the fact that I was trans.

"You're just a butch lesbian," she would always say. *"Why don't you get over yourself and admit it? This trans stuff is just a phase. It's just the latest trend."*

Except it wasn't trendy. Being a trans man is part of who and what I am. I wasn't going to let her take that from me. Not again.

Watching as my boyfriend struggled to release Marsha from Vyviane's grip, I swallowed down the bile rising from my gullet. I would not throw up. I would not give her the satisfaction. No. Instead I whipped a clean handkerchief from my pocket, blotted my face, and took in a deep breath.

The whole time John was still struggling with her, Vyviane kept her eyes trained on me. She didn't seem to care about John, or Marsha P. Johnson fighting for her life, or the fact that Klaus barked at her ankles and looked about to bite her at any moment.

Time moved in slow motion. Sweetheart Digs smirked, arms crossed over his chest. Every table in that courtyard was staring, looking at the scene Vyviane was causing. And still she wouldn't give up her hold on Marsha, who yelped in anger and distress.

Vyviane always did like scenes. Just as much as I hated being the center of attention, she thrived on it.

I calmly folded my handkerchief, placed it carefully back in my pocket, squared my shoulders, and looked back into her eyes. Once upon a time, I thought her eyes were beautiful, but now I could see how cold and calculating and greedy she was.

"Give me back my dog, Vyviane." My words were measured. Calm.

"Oh, is this your puppy? She's very cute."

"Give her back, Vyviane."

"Awww," she said, pouting. "But she likes me."

Marsha snapped at her face again, barely missing Vyviane's perfect little nose. The corgi's eyes rolled in panic. That was it.

I lunged forward and grabbed Marsha's collar just as John got a hand beneath her paws. I wrapped my other arm around Marsha's furry little body, and the two of us pulled as Klaus barked down below.

Marsha popped like a cork out of Vyviane's arms, little paws scrabbling in the air. I clutched her to my chest, and she licked my face in gratitude. That made me feel better.

John snapped his fingers for Klaus, who obediently rushed to sit at his heels. John picked up Klaus's leash, making sure Vyviane couldn't get to him, either.

"What do you want, Vyviane?" I asked.

"Just to see you. Is that so wrong?"

"What's the matter? Did the country musicians decide they didn't like you very much? Or did that oil mogul I heard you sank your talons into finally give you the boot? That's a common thing for you, isn't it? People not liking you? Did you run out of money, tuck tail and come home?"

The words poured out of me like poison. Vyviane's mouth set in a grim, angry line, and for a moment, she looked as if she would spit.

Then I watched her transform. She shimmied her shoulders as if shaking off her anger, and quickly smiled again.

"So, everything all right here?" Daniel stepped up next to Vyviane.

"Just some old friends having a chat," she said. "And how are you, Daniel?"

"Doing well, Vyviane. Let me know if you need anything." He gave me another glare and backed away, but I noticed he touched Vyviane's arm as he did so. He touched her in a way that seemed far too familiar. What was happening? Were Daniel and Vyviane dating?

As far as I knew, Daniel only liked men. Vyviane called herself pansexual, but since she didn't like trans people, I didn't see how that was possible. But she at least had a history of dating both women and men. But Daniel? I never knew he swung any way other than gay.

"Are you two working together?" John asked, eyes narrowed.

Daniel stopped and laughed nervously.

"Of course not. What makes you think that? I just, you know… I just know Vyviane from a long time ago, don't I, Viv?"

She smiled and said nothing. Something fishy was definitely going on.

"I think I'm done with my dinner, John," I said. "How about you?"

He nodded. "Yeah. Hey, Daniel," he called to the owner's receding back. "Can we please get our check?"

Vyviane stepped closer. Both Marsha and Klaus growled deep in their throats. Good dogs. She paused.

"I really need to talk to you, Garrett." Her voice was suddenly urgent.

I looked her up and down. Her attractive slender figure, her perfect jeans and perfect makeup. The single tasteful silver strand around her pale and perfect neck.

How had I ever found her attractive? How had I ever fallen in love?

"Whatever you need, Vyviane," I replied, "you're not going to get it from me."

I turned away, Marsha still held in my arms. Then I turned back. Vyviane still stood there, as if waiting for something.

"I don't want anything from you, Vyviane. And I don't think you want anything from me, at least not that I'm willing to give. I gave too much to you already."

She started to speak, but I held up a hand.

"But know this: If you had anything to do with Saschi's death, I will come to get you. I will gladly hunt you down."

Klaus, bless his furry little heart, growled, and Marsha barked three times as if in warning.

Vyviane's face looked like she was sucking on a lemon. She turned and stalked out of the courtyard.

I sagged in relief.

John put an arm around me. "You did good, babe. You did really, really, well. But you owe me the story now."

"Thanks," I said. "And you owe me one about Sweetheart Digs."

"Fair enough."

But as I stared after that cloud of blonde hair, I couldn't help but wonder what in the world Vyviane was up to.

And I had a feeling we were about to find out.

CHAPTER 28

Adam

I'D BEEN PACING the rooms of the beautiful old house. Garrett really did have a way with design. The furniture was a mix of contemporary and Mission style, but it all blended to match the original Craftsman bones of the home.

Garrett had brought a box home from the shop. I'd slowly been rifling through it while the house was quiet. Slowly, because it takes a lot of effort and concentration to move anything. Luckily, it was mostly paper, and that stuff was light.

What I'd found was disturbing, though, and matched the snatches of conversation I'd picked up on between Garrett and John, and what the corgis had told me.

Their dead waiter had been quite the blackmailer. But there was one letter that had gotten stuck to the sides of the box. A letter they needed to see.

So, I paced until they got home, boots tracing patterns on the floors that not even I could see. Finally, I heard the scrabble of doggie toenails on the front porch, a key in the old lock, and the two men and corgis burst in, clearly in an uproar.

Something had happened to upset them.

"I can't believe the nerve of her," John said, as he unhooked both dogs from their leashes and kicked off his shoes.

Garrett sighed and pulled his own shoes off more slowly. Both men neatly put them on the wood rack by the door.

Klaus and Marsha bounded up to me, sniffing at my boots, then racing away and back again. They raced between me, Garrett, John, and the front windows, then made the circuit once again.

"What's up, my corgi friends?" I asked.

"The bad woman was at the restaurant!" Klaus barked. "She tried to kidnap Marsha!"

I looked from the reddish tan and white corgi to his mostly black friend.

"Marsha?"

"Not kidnapped, exactly. But she was holding me pretty tight and wouldn't let go. Even when I kicked."

"What did she want?"

"She threatened Garrett!" Klaus's little brow wrinkled. "At least, I think she did. Humans are so confusing."

"Can you two settle down a little?" Garrett asked. He sounded weary. Wrung out.

John kissed his forehead. "I'll make us a cup of tea. You sit down, okay?"

Garrett nodded and John headed to the kitchen.

::I found something,:: I said to Marsha. ::You need to make Garrett look at the paper on the table next to the box, okay?::

Marsha woofed her assent and trotted into the dining room. She placed her paws on a wood dining chair and began nosing around the box.

Garrett didn't sit in the living room. Instead, he followed Marsha to the table and plopped down in a dining room chair, reaching out to scratch behind Marsha's ears. Klaus trundled over beside me and looked up, tongue lolling, panting happily.

While Marsha still looked worried, Klaus seemed to roll with the punches more easily.

"What's up, girl?" Garrett asked. "Are you okay after all that?"

Marsha whined and pawed at the table.

"Hey." Garrett put a hand on her paw. "Stop that. You'll scratch the surface, and the last thing I want is to have to sand and restain this piece."

He wasn't getting it. Not yet. I drifted closer, leaning over him, and felt the small man shiver.

Marsha barked at me. "He's not looking, Adam. Can you do something?"

Garrett followed Marsha's gaze until he was staring right at me. Or he would have been, if he could see me. As it was, he looked through me, which felt a little disconcerting.

"Adam?" he asked. "Are you here?"

Then he turned back to Marsha, who pawed at the table again.

"Is that who you're seeing? The ghost?" He frowned down at her paw. "Stop pawing at the table! What are you…"

I felt the change in him when Garrett saw the paper. He slowly reached for it.

"How did this get out of the box? Marsha? Did you do this?" His fair head swiveled from the corgi and back to the general area where he thought I was. "Or was it you?"

If I still breathed, the breath would have caught in my throat. Having a human being speak directly to me like this filled me with a strange emotion. The only other time the men had spoken to me was when Klaus and Marsha first found me. The men had barely noticed me since.

It felt good to be noticed. I had missed it. Being a ghost is lonely, I realized. But enough wool gathering.

I softly touched Garrett's hand. He gasped and pulled it away.

"It is you," he said.

I fluttered the edges of the paper. He nodded as if he understood, and pulling it all the way toward him, he began to read.

"John?" he called into the kitchen.

"Yes?" John returned, holding two steaming mugs of tea. I missed warm drinks. Not so much drinking them but holding them. I'd give anything to absorb some warmth again.

Marsha gave me a short bark, as if she heard my thoughts. I smiled down at the little black corgi, with her tan and white makeup.

"Look what I found," Garrett said. "Or what Marsha and the ghost found."

John set the mugs on two coasters, then leaned over Garrett, one hand on his partner's shoulder. I missed that, too. The easy intimacy of being around people I loved.

I'd come to love the corgis and these men, and I think the corgis, at least, loved me back. But I missed my own dog, Lucy. And I missed my former housemates, and my lovers, long since dead.

Just like me.

John gave a low whistle. "Well. This changes every-thing, doesn't it?"

Garrett nodded.

"Did you suspect?" John asked.

"I did. But I have a whole list of suspects, and other people were a lot higher on the list."

I waited, so did Marsha and Klaus. John pulled out a chair and sat. Both men blew across the surface of their tea, deep in thought.

The refrigerator turned over and hummed from the kitchen. Klaus dragged a bone over from his bed and settled in to quietly gnaw. Marsha, though?

She clearly wanted to move this thing along and nosed her head into Garrett's leg. He absentmindedly reached down to pat her head. She gave a slight woof, but Garrett didn't reply.

Finally, John spoke again. "What are we going to do about it?"

Track the person down and make them pay, was my first thought. But I was always a bit of a hothead, wasn't I? It worked well for me when I needed to chain myself to a light rail train, blockade City Hall, or throw red paint at a pharmaceutical company's local offices.

But other times? Giving in to my quick temper wasn't always the best move.

"We're going to throw a party," Garrett said. "In Saschi's honor. Ask every single person we know in Pride Street to come."

Marsha barked.

John sat still for a moment, as if shell shocked. Then he grinned.

"You beautiful, beautiful genius!" He grabbed Garrett's face in both hands and gave him a swift kiss.

When they broke apart, both men were smiling.

It was a wonderful thing to see.

CHAPTER 29
Garrett

TONIGHT WAS THE NIGHT. The café looked terrific. Jacki had found a good photo of Saschi and blown it up. It sat on a stand between two vases filled with a variety of bright flowers. Nothing funereal here.

Cookies, cheese and crackers, and an assortment of sodas, beer, and wine festooned tables on either side of the photo. To get a snack, you had to do so under Saschi's watchful gaze. That should shake a few people up. Or put them off their cheese.

Now we just needed to wait for people to arrive.

Turns out, throwing a party takes a lot of work. What do I know about throwing parties? I'm an introvert. The only parties we've had at the house have all been organized and kept running by John.

We'd debated where to have the thing, finally asking Bex and Jacki if they would host it at the café after closing. Once I told them our plan, they swiftly agreed. I designed fliers while John made phone calls.

We had to make it look as if the party really was just a neighborhood-wide memorial, and not like we were trying to gather all our suspects in one spot.

The dogs and I had wandered, stapling and taping fliers up everywhere. John had talked personally with the most important people, and assured me my list of suspects were all on board. Some of them reluctantly, of course, but John had a way of subtly pressuring people into doing exactly what he wanted.

I'm really glad he's a writer and not some self-help mogul, because otherwise, he'd be dangerous.

As it was, I think some of the primary invitees decided that to not show up would be suspicious, which was exactly as I'd hoped. I wanted people on their toes.

"Nervous?"

I jumped at Bex's voice. She smiled at me from behind the counter.

"That obvious, huh?"

But she didn't have time to answer. A gaggle of queens waltzed in, waving fans and hankies, heels clattering on the café floor.

"Oh! Look at these sweet dogs!" one of the queens crooned, and soon Bruiser, Marsha, and Klaus were all being fawned over.

Sweetheart Digs walked in next, still sockless, in a silver blazer and those garish silver loafers. Daniel and Vyviane followed closely behind, though they didn't seem to be speaking with each other.

Vyviane looked like she wanted to come over, but John squared his shoulders at my side and stared her off.

"She has some nerve," he murmured. I had to agree.

Other neighborhood people filtered in. Jacki put on

some techno music—Saschi's favorite—and the beers were cracked, wine was opened, and the conversation volume slowly rose.

Ron arrived next, with Fred ambling slowly at his side and Josephine Baker perched on his shoulder. He had thrown a black blazer on over his Bones, Dogs, and Harmony T-shirt. I hoped Josephine Baker had good sphincter control, or that Ron's dry cleaner was able to get parrot poop out of lightweight summer wool.

Ron waved in greeting as Fred, black tail wagging, headed over to the other dogs.

Ace and Jerome from Enrico's walked in, followed by the man himself. I kicked myself for not questioning him, but he'd proven to be slippery. But since stealing was his issue and not blackmail, I had struck him from the suspect list anyway.

Speaking of suspects, Tomaso, Roderick, and Princess Sparkle Toes waltzed in, forming an odd trio, especially as I thought Roderick was still mad at Sparkle Toes. Everyone was dressed in their best finery, whether that meant clean jeans and a vest with extra jewelry, or fancy frocks and suits.

The food remained untouched, but the beer and wine were flowing. I guess Saschi's portrait put people off their food, but not their drink.

I nursed a soda water with lime, wanting to keep my head clear. John circulated, greeting people and doing what he did best. Bex and Jacki did the same. All three of them were eavesdropping as they went. I held up the counter, glass in hand. I needed to anchor myself for a while, or I would never get through this.

Finally, Yarrow walked in, looking red eyed and tentative. They were still dressed in black, with the exception of their trademark rainbow shoes. The yellow on their short cap of curls looked freshly dyed and makeup made their cheekbones look even higher than they already were.

Yarrow looked around, seeming a bit overwhelmed, saw Saschi's portrait, and teared up.

John caught my eye, and we approached them from opposite sides of the room. I gently touched Yarrow's arm.

"You okay?" John asked.

They nodded yes, sniffed, and we all pretended it was true.

"You ready for this?" I asked.

They released a hissing sigh. "Not really. I know we talked about the whole plan last night, but are you sure?"

Yarrow's eyes darted nervously around the now full café. They weren't the only nervous one. Other eyes cut toward us, then away. Good. Some of these people needed to sweat.

Then I remembered the button I'd tucked into my pocket that morning. "Yarrow, is this yours?"

I held out the retro *Still Here, Still Queer* pin. Yarrow's eyes lit up.

"I wondered where that had gone. Thank you!"

I could tell from Yarrow's eyes they really meant it.

"Saschi gave it to me a couple of years ago. Found it in some vintage store." Yarrow pinned it to their flowing black overshirt, and gave it a pat.

Jacki approached.

"Ready to get this party started? Just say the word, and I'll turn the music down."

John gave my hand a squeeze, and I looked at Yarrow, who dabbed their eyes and nodded.

"Yeah," I said. "I think we're ready."

Ready as we'd ever be to read out loud a letter written by a dead person and found by a dog and a ghost.

CHAPTER 30

Marsha

"WHAT DO *you think is going to happen?"* Bruiser asked in between wheezes. I swear, I have sympathy for the bulldog, but sometimes listening to him is painful.

"Garrett is going to bite the bad person!" Klaus yapped.

I sighed. *"Garrett is not going to bite anyone."*

But he was going to get someone in big trouble. Maybe even a time out.

I turned to Bruiser and Fred, who waited patiently. We were all grouped around a table not too far from the human snacks. I kept hoping someone would drop a piece of cheese, but so far the only casualty had been a carrot stick that a person in high heels had almost tripped over.

The café was crowded with people's legs and shoes, which made it kind of hard to see, but there was a break between a couple of groups, and I saw Garrett conferring with Jacki. Pretty soon, the music lowered.

"I think he's going to read the letter Adam found now," I said.

Sure enough, conversation slowly petered out, just as Jacki raised her arms.

She looked pretty today. A yellow scarf wrapped around her forehead, framing her short curly hair, and gold earrings dangled from her ears.

"Thank you all for coming," she said. "Many of us knew and loved Saschi... even when they got on our last nerve."

People laughed at that, but it wasn't the real kind of laughter humans sometimes make when they're happy. This laughter sounded kind of sad.

"Saschi was a good waiter, a good friend, and a notorious gossip who loved to spill the tea! That's why we have a lot of tea on the tables, along with the cookies, cheese, beer, and wine. If you don't like the tea, you can always get drunk on sugar or booze. Just know we'll kick you out if you get sloppy!"

Jacki was smiling to show people she was kidding. But I didn't think she really was. Dogs were so much more straightforward than humans. We meant what we said, and said what we meant. And if we didn't like you? We'd just pee on your shoes.

"There will be time to share memories of Saschi, but first, Garrett would like to read something. Garrett?"

Garrett straightened his bow tie, swallowed, and then nodded. John squeezed his arm, then Garrett took two steps forward, cleared his throat, and unfolded a piece of paper.

"I'd like to read you something I found in Saschi's things. Yarrow was kind enough to collect a box for Saschi's family and friends. You'll have noticed some of their jewelry and pins and a few odds and ends laid out on the tables in the back there. If you knew Saschi, feel free to take something as a memento."

People shifted nervously, looking at each other. I smelled some fear, along with the sugar and beer.

And roses.

"Klaus!"

"What?"

"Do you smell roses?"

John motioned at us to hush before Klaus could answer. I grumbled a little, but settled on my hind legs, waiting to see what happened next.

Garrett took a sip of water from a glass, then set it down. He seemed really nervous. Maybe he needed help. I sidled up to him and pressed my shoulder against his leg.

He looked down and smiled, then looked back at the people, scanning their faces, before looking back down at the paper.

"I'll just read this, then. Pretty soon, you'll know why. It's a photocopy of a letter Saschi wrote before they died. Unlike most of us, Saschi was a romantic who still believed in sending cards and letters. And the important ones? They kept a copy for themselves. I don't know why, exactly, but several letters were in the box, along with notes and cards Saschi had received from friends."

And people who weren't Saschi's friends, too. Just like the note that threatened me.

Everyone hushed. The only sounds were Bruiser's breathing, some noise from the street, and the occasional tinkle as someone moved and their bracelets knocked against each other.

"I always loved you," Garrett began reading, "and I probably always will. Even after what you did. Stupid, I know. But a person can't always change what their heart decides. You were cruel to so many people, including me. But you were also bright, and beautiful, and could make me feel adored. That said, the thing you did is inexcusable. Princess Sparkle Toes did not deserve that treatment, even if she can sometimes be a bitch."

"Bad word! Bad word!" Josephine Baker squawked from Ron's shoulder.

Sparkle Toes gasped and moved forward, but Ron grabbed her before she could snatch the letter out of Garrett's hands.

"You stole something precious from her. A thing that she can never get back. I've decided I'm going to tell her all about it next time I see her. We're having tea tomorrow afternoon. You have until then to clear things up and make amends."

Princess Sparkle Toes was sobbing by this time. Ron had an arm wrapped around her, keeping her upright.

"I don't understand," one of the queens asked. "Who is Saschi writing to?"

I looked up at Garrett. He looked down at me. "You want to tell them, Marsha P?"

"Come, on!" Sweetheart Digs burst. "Your dog is going to tell us what you're talking about? I thought we were here to honor Saschi, not listen to some melodrama!"

"Your presence is melodrama enough for us all, you old fraud," Daniel said, voice dry.

"Now hear this!" Sweetheart started toward Daniel, hands outstretched as if he was going to choke the restauranteur.

Ace put her fingers between her lips and whistled loud enough to hurt my ears.

"Stop it!" The bartender yelled. "All of you! Saschi is dead and Garrett is about to tell us who killed them. Aren't you, Garrett?"

"Then get on with it," Enrico said. "Some of us have work to get to tonight."

"Marsha?" Garrett spoke without looking at me, just as a scuffle broke out. Someone was running for the door.

"*All dogs to the door!*" I barked. The four of us charged through the crowd and blocked the entryway just as Roderick skidded to a halt.

CHAPTER 31

Garrett

"YOU?" Princess Sparkle Toes was aghast. "You killed Saschi?"

Ace and Bex each held one of Roderick's arms as the dogs all growled and snapped around his legs. He struggled but was no match for the two women.

Yarrow stalked through the shocked clumps of people and slapped Roderick across the face, hard enough that his head snapped sideways. Then Yarrow burst into tears. Ron tugged on her shoulder and led her away. Yarrow fell into Princess Sparkle Toe's arms, and they cried together. But I noticed PST's eyes never left Roderick. Beneath her tears was a spark of anger.

"Roderick?" I asked, moving closer, John still glued to my side.

Tears streamed down his face, and he could barely lift his eyes to look at me.

"You don't understand. They were blackmailing me! They were blackmailing so many people!" He turned toward Princess Sparkle Toes, who lifted her chin and patted Yarrow on the back protectively.

"I shouldn't have taken those things from you! But you hurt me, and I wanted to hurt you back. By the time Saschi found out about it, I had sold most of the things."

"Why, Roderick? Why did you have to sell them?" PST looked stricken now.

"Because I lost my job. I needed some help to pay the bills until I found a new one."

Until he started his new career, he meant.

"And why did you murder Saschi?" I asked.

He turned his gaze on me. "Saschi was right. Princess Sparkle Toes didn't deserve my treatment of her. But Saschi? That bitch. I didn't mean to kill them, I swear! I really didn't! I just thought I'd put a scare into them. Get their heart racing a bit, you know? I wanted to make Saschi sweat, the way they'd made me sweat. Literally. It was simple enough to shake a little liquid nicotine on that mint gum they constantly chewed, greedy cow."

"Simple enough, and deadly," John murmured.

"What about the roses?" Marsha barked.

John shushed her. But as I stared at Roderick, I realized something else was bothering me.

I looked over to where Daniel and Vyviane still stood together. Not like lovers, I realized, but like co-conspirators.

"How about you two? What did you have to do with all of this?"

Vyviane pasted an innocent *who me?* look on her pretty face, while Daniel drew himself up, mouth set in a determined line.

"Saschi threatened me," he said, "and Vyviane came up

with a way to get back at them. But I couldn't be seen near the locker where Saschi kept their stuff. Vyviane pretended to get lost on her way to the washrooms and planted a note in Saschi's bag, threatening them. You know, like an *I know what you did last summer* sort of thing. I know it's petty—" he shrugged "—but Saschi was really getting under my skin."

So that second note, the one not in the black envelope? The one that read "I know what you did?" That must have been planted by Vyviane. I stared at my former girlfriend, disgusted. It was as if I didn't know her at all.

Maybe someday I'd find out what she was doing back and what she wanted from me, but today was not that day. Right now I just wished she had never returned.

Then Yarrow paled two shades, fingers clutching the pin on their shirt. "Oh, my good Goddess!"

"What?" asked Princess Sparkle Toes.

"I… I had borrowed some nicotine gum from Saschi a few months ago and finally slipped replacements in their bag a week ago, as a surprise. I mixed them in with the plastic jar of gum they had in their bag."

I looked at Yarrow, confused, and I wasn't the only one.

Yarrow explained. "Saschi mixed the nicotine gum in with regular mint gum as a way to help the flavor. They chewed them two at a time, saying the harder they chewed, the less they wanted to smoke."

"But Saschi had quit the nicotine gum," Daniel said. "They were proud of it. They were still chewing those disgusting double chiclets of gum, insisting on doing so even while on shift. No customer wants to watch their waiter chewing a wad of gum. Saschi looked like a cow, chewing cud! I had stern words with Saschi about it, but they ignored me. Said it was better than smoking, so I shouldn't complain."

Wow. This had swerved an unexpected direction. I reached out and grabbed John's hand.

"So, it was the double dose of nicotine that killed Saschi," Sparkle Toes said. "The liquid and the gum. Does this mean their death was an accident?"

Everyone looked at me, as if I was supposed to form a ruling. I shook my head. Figuring out Roderick's involvement had been enough. I didn't need to sentence anybody.

Sweetheart Digs cleared his throat. "I think, as a community, we can probably rule this an accident. But the fact still remains that Roderick deliberately added liquid nicotine to Saschi's gum. He intended Saschi harm, even if he didn't mean to kill them."

Roderick broke into heaving, gusty sobs.

"And Saschi intended a lot of us harm, too," murmured Princess Sparkle Toes.

Wasn't that the truth?

CHAPTER 32

Marsha

MOST OF THE humans had left. John and Ron helped Bex and Jacki clean up the café while Sweetheart Digs packed up the extra food to take to a homeless shelter.

I guess he's not always a jerk. Just most of the time.

Garrett sat at one of the tables, talking quietly with Yarrow and Roderick. As far as I was concerned, Roderick deserved a big bite on the ankles, but it seemed like the humans weren't so sure.

"I don't understand why Roderick isn't being punished," I whined. *"I mean, there are good dogs and bad dogs, and bad dogs need to know what they've done wrong."*

Bruiser snorted, and Klaus tilted his head and flicked his ears, as if thinking. But it was Fred who finally spoke.

"A bad dog isn't always bad," he whuffed.

I looked at the black lab, tilting my own head in confusion. *"What do you mean?"*

"A bad dog is sometimes just a mistreated dog. Sometimes a little kindness is all a dog needs to be good."

Then the older dog rose and walked slowly over to

Ron, who looked down and patted his head. Josephine Baker squawked something rude, as usual, but settled down pretty quickly once Ron stroked her gray head, too.

"*Do you think Fred is right?*" Klaus asked me.

I wasn't sure. Fred was usually right, though. I always thought of him as a wise old dog. But…

"*I don't know. But I want to think about it some more. Maybe Saschi was mean to other humans because Saschi was mistreated, too.*"

Bruiser drooled on the floor, then woofed. "*I think Fred is right. I was a runt. All the other pups in my litter picked on me, until I learned to fight back and defend my food. And no one wanted to adopt me because my underbite was too big, and I was so growly, especially at mealtimes. It took Bex and Jacki two months to get me to settle down and trust them. I used to whine and snap at anyone who got close.*"

I had no idea. Bruiser was such a chill dog. I couldn't imagine him snapping at anyone. Like I said, he's even scared of bees.

"*Huh,*" I said. "*It just goes to show you, you can't always tell what's going on inside a person, dog or human.*"

"*Can we get treats now?*" Klaus asked, jumping to his feet. "*We were promised treats.*"

"*Good idea!*"

Klaus was right. In all the human drama, our treats had gone undelivered.

We all headed toward Bex and Jacki, barking up a storm. They laughed and broke out the dog cookies.

Even Garrett smiled from his corner table, though Yarrow and Roderick still looked pretty sad.

CHAPTER 33

Garrett

I LAY in bed next to John, who was reading quietly. I was too restless to read. The dogs both snored softly on their big bed under the window.

"Well," I said, "that was exhausting. Remind me to never have to go through an ordeal like that again."

John closed the giant hardback resting against his blanket-covered knees. It was some sort of thriller with a lurid cover. I sometimes teased him about having a busman's holiday, writing thrillers and mysteries, and reading the same. He always replied that he read plenty of romance, history, and science fiction, too.

And he was right. A well-rounded man, my partner.

"You doing okay?" he asked.

"Not really. I mean, what was all this for? So much pain spread around so many people, and for what? And now Saschi is dead because of one person's mistake and someone else's attempt at revenge."

John looked across our bedroom, as if thinking.

"It feels like the whole community is paying for Saschi's crimes. And Roderick's, too."

That was exactly it. Too many people were paying for the actions of a few. But wasn't that the way of the world?

I sighed and snuggled against John's shoulder. His T-shirt was soft and smelled of lavender laundry soap, his special John scent, and home.

He wrapped an arm around me, pulling me closer, and we both snuggled deeper under the covers, laying quietly for a while.

"It's pretty weird that the ghost is the one who found that letter Saschi sent to Roderick. You think I should thank him?"

I felt John's head nod. "Probably so. Think he's in the room with us?"

My eyes scanned the dressers, the art on the walls, and the old wood window casings, finally lighting on the closet doors. It was a little unsettling to know that the ghost of a 1980s leather daddy could be watching us.

"Adam?" I asked the room. "You there?"

The closet door slowly creaked open. A shiver crossed over my bare forearms and Marsha woke and gave a soft bark, the kind she gave for friends.

"Guess that's your answer," John whispered.

"Adam, I hope you know you're welcome in our home. Uh…your home. Sorry. Not used to talking to ghosts. At any rate, thanks for your help on the case. We couldn't have done it without you."

Both Klaus and Marsha yipped at that. I smiled.

"Or Marsha and Klaus, either. Thanks, all three of you."

Then I turned to John, who was smiling down at me.

"And thanks for being my partner. You are awesome."

He gave me a soft kiss. "You're pretty awesome yourself."

"Oh yeah? How about you prove it to me?"

He laughed again and drew me closer. The closet door squeaked shut, and the dogs settled back on their bed.

And that's all she wrote.

CHAPTER 34

Adam

ALL WAS WELL with the world again. Or at least this little part of it. I was pleased to have been able to help out, in my own, small, ghostly way. Sure, it wasn't dramatic, like occupying the offices of a multinational pharmaceutical company, or chaining myself to the light rail with my friends, but it was help all the same.

And one thing I've learned, being dead?

Sometimes it's the small things that are most important in life.

Small acts of kindness, and love. The smell of coffee. The laughter of friends. And two men and their dogs, falling to sleep, knowing they did what they could to keep their community safe.

We all take care of each other as best we can. As Klaus Nomi once said, "We all live on this planet. We're all living on the earth."

That would be the human performer, Klaus Nomi, not the tan and white corgi currently sleeping in the dog bed with his best friend.

At any rate, the human Klaus Nomi was right. We share this spinning planet with each other and forget it at our peril. All the fighting and backbiting, all the jealousy and strife?

At the end of the day, it doesn't much matter.

What matters is that we do our best by each other, living or dead.

We do our best, and try to have some good times along the way.

THERE'S trouble among the mums and lilies at Pride Street's favorite florist. The flower shop cat, Sapphire has gone missing! Danger stalks the streets, the Pride Street animals are in an uproar, and the trouble isn't over yet. Klaus and Marsha are on the case…

Find out what happens next, in Flower Frenzy!

And more...

If you enjoyed this book, please consider telling a friend, or leaving a short review at your favorite booksellers. Many thanks!

And visit thorncoyle.com to sign up for a weekly newsletter.

Acknowledgments

A big thank you and yip, yip, hurrah to my Kickstarter backers! Thanks also to my Patreon supporters who were the first to read about Marsha, Klaus, and Adam the ghost. I'm eternally grateful for your support!

Thank you to Bonnie for reading, to Annie for editing, to Morpheus and Juniper the Corgi for sharing their corgi expertise. And always, to my chosen family for your years of support.

Most of all, thank you to everyone who fell in love with two men and their dogs and the queer little village-in-a-city they call home.

FICTION

Seashell Cove Paranormal Cozy Mysteries

Bookshop Witch

Haunted Witch

Tarot Witch

Running Witch

Hallows Witch

The Pride Street Paranormal Cozy Mysteries

Sushi Scandal

Flower Frenzy

Muffin Murder

Hairspray Horror

Dandy Distress

The Witches of Portland (complete)

By Earth

By Flame

By Wind

By Sea

By Moon

By Sun

By Dusk

By Dark

By Witch's Mark

The Panther Chronicles (Complete)

To Raise a Clenched Fist to the Sky

To Wrest Our Bodies From the Fire

To Drown This Fury in the Sea

To Stand With Power on This Ground

The Steel Clan Saga

We Seek No Kings

We Heed No Laws

We Ride at Night

Short Story Collections

A Hint of Faery

A Touch of Faery

A Spark of Magic

A Flame for Yuletide

A Hope for Winter

A Time for Magic

A Speculation of Stars

A Speculation of Hope

Risk It All: Queer Stories of Love, Suspense, And Daring

Thresholds: Queer Stories of Love, Suspense, And Daring

NON-FICTION

Evolutionary Witchcraft

Kissing the Limitless

Make Magic of Your Life

Sigil Magic for Writers, Artists & Other Creatives

Crafting a Daily Practice

Resistance Matters

About the Author

T. Thorn Coyle worked in many strange and diverse occupations before settling in to write novels. Buy them a cup of tea and perhaps they'll tell you about it.

Author of the *Seashell Cove Paranormal Cozy Mystery* series, the *Pride Street Paranormal Cozy Mystery* series, *The Witches of Portland*, *The Steel Clan Saga*, and *The Panther Chronicles*, Thorn's multiple non-fiction books include *Sigil Magic for Writers, Artists & Other Creatives*, and *Evolutionary Witchcraft*.

Thorn's work appears in many anthologies, magazines, and collections. They have taught magical practice in nine countries, on four continents, and in twenty-five states.

An interloper to the Pacific Northwest U.S., Thorn stalks city streets and talks to crows, squirrels, and trees.

Connect with Thorn:
www.thorncoyle.com

www.ingramcontent.com/pod-product-compliance
Lightning Source LLC
Chambersburg PA
CBHW070504200726

48293CB00007B/2383